Silver Stirrups

Silver Wind Equine Rescue Romance

Susan Lower

Time Glider
Books

Susan Lower
Visit my website at www.susanlower.com

Printed in the United States of America

First Printing: November 2019
Time Glider Books, LLC

ISBN: 978-19452740-0-8

For everyone who asks, receives, and he who seeks, finds; and to him who knocks, it will be opened.

LUKE 11:10

Chapter One

A few days after Alison Vandergraft's grandfather took a spill out on the trail with his horse, she stood in the stables staring into an empty stall. Warm temperatures in the middle of February made the ice shift, and the melted snow turned the trails and the pastures of Windy Knoll Farms into a mess.

Alison arrived early, assuring Gramps she'd take care of the stables and all the horses boarded there as part of the Silver Stirrups Riding Club. She paused by the empty stall, resting her hand on the bars of the sliding door; cold to the touch, it sent a chill straight to her soul.

She couldn't remember the last time she'd come here and hadn't tripped over the little flutter of hope she learned to ignore as the days passed. Inside the stall, the scent of oats and clean sawdust mocked her. She left the stall door unlocked, as it had been the morning she came to check on her beloved Leopard Appaloosa, Gus.

Someone stole him right out of the pasture.

And deep down, she suspected who.

But she couldn't prove it.

She had to believe Gus was somewhere safe. Somewhere loved.

He'd been gone for a long time: four months, six days, and counting.

Beside the empty stall, a horse nickered, pulling Alison out of her mini pity party. She promised Gramps she'd see to his horse. Otherwise, she feared the elderly cowboy would have tried to check out of the hospital without the doctor releasing him.

Grabbing the lead and sliding open the door, Alison held her hand out to the pretty sorrel mare. "Easy, girl. Do you think you can step out here for me? We'll get you cleaned up and ready for the doc."

Mud caked the animal's hide. Gramps's friend Randy had washed and wrapped the front leg, which had swelled with the injury. Slowly, Alison gave the horse a little tug and let the mare come out on her own, limping and stepping out into the aisle. "A few more steps. That's a girl."

Alison clipped the crossties on the horse's halter and left the horse to stand while she gathered some supplies. Randy might have tended to the horse's wounds, but cleaning off the mud had been the least of all their worries. Gramps would spit nails to see a horse not properly tended.

Outside she heard the truck pull up.

"I'll be back," she told the horse. Remembering how Gus would toss his head in agreement with whatever she would say, her heart skipped a beat waiting, but Gramps's horse paid no attention to her. She sighed and went to greet the veterinarian.

"Morning."

"Good morning." Alison glanced over at the most handsome face she'd ever seen. It made her forget her manners and left her tongue-tied to say anything back.

Since when could a man's face make her forget her words? Not any face, Josh Anderson's face. The one guy back in high school who caught her interest.

Dr. Michael Kingsley strolled into the barn. After a brief introduction, he asked, "How is your grandfather?"

Alison hurried to lead the way to where the mare stood. With every step, she scolded herself to get it together. She and Josh had gone out a few times before the end of her junior year in high school. That summer, he'd gone away to work as a groom and forgot about her when he returned. She had long gotten over the way he ignored her when he came back that last year in school. Alison had to laugh to relieve the nerves building inside her and tried to push the past behind her. People did stupid things in high school.

Some more than others.

She took hold of Mistress's halter, as Dr. Kingsley approached.

"He's still as ornery as ever. But it will be a while before he can get back up on his mistress here." She patted the horse's neck. Her grandfather raised Mistress from a foal. Her grandmother had teased she was his second lady, so he named her Mistress. The sorrel mare nickered at the sound of her name.

Josh leaned against the stall door. Last she heard he skipped college and made a living hauling horses and working over at the Silver Wind Equine Rescue. "Sorry he got hurt."

Alison couldn't seem to make her voice work when it came to speaking, which made her all the more anxious for the veterinarian to take a look at Mistress and her injured leg. She managed to swallow down these silly schoolgirl vibes blocking her voice and said, "Thanks."

Dr. Kingsley spoke softly to the horse, ran his hand down the injured leg. Mistress stepped back away from the veterinarian's touch. "It's hot and swollen."

Dr. Kingsley kept one hand on the horse and spoke while he unwrapped the dressing around the mare's legs. "She tripped out on the trail?"

3

"Gramps was leading a group out through the pasture, and Mistress dropped her foot down in a groundhog hole. With the mud and the snow and the grass, well, you can imagine neither horse nor man saw it," Alison said.

When Dr. Michael Kingsley straightened up, the expression on his face caused a pang of sorrow. She leaned closer to Mistress. She knew before he said it. Alison's heart reached clear to the hospital where her grandfather rested and waited for word on his mistress.

"It's broken, isn't it?"

"There's no doubt. She's not putting any weight on it," Dr. Kingsley said.

"How bad is it?" Josh moved closer. "The bone's not coming out. Can't you cast it and let it heal?"

Dr. Kingsley shook his head. "If it were a clean break or a fracture, but —" He ran his hand back down, the horse shied away, and Dr. Kingsley winced. Looking up at Alison, he said, "There are pieces of bone floating around here, by the joint."

Alison's hands trembled. "We can't lose Mistress."

Josh moved close to her. His eyes had lost their playful spark she remembered from high school. He stood close, too close. She could smell the leather and mixed grasses of hay, along with the other horses, and drew comfort from it. How would Gramps cope without Mistress?

They couldn't afford to lose another horse, not with Gus gone, and a horse short since they took on more senior riders to the club last month.

Alison placed a hand on her heart, a silent prayer for strength, and that miracle Randy mentioned behind her lips. If God willed it, He could heal Mistress and Gramps, and bring Gus back. One thing at a time. Alison took a deep breath. Mistress rubbed against her shoulder.

"An older horse like Mistress, I could wrap it up, keep her off the foot, but with those pieces floating around, it'll cause her pain."

"I don't want her to be in pain. I know Gramps won't either, but I need to talk to him first."

Josh's hand laid on her shoulder and squeezed gently. "Course you do."

"Either way, I wouldn't take the mare out on the trail again. I'd have to take an X-ray to see how bad it is, but it would be best to end her pain." Dr. Kingsley glanced over at Josh and gave him a nod to go. Looking back at Alison, he said, "You let me know what your grandfather decides. It needs to be soon if we're going to try and fix the leg. I'd rather have her at the clinic and do X-rays."

Those weren't the words her grandfather would want to hear. "Gramps won't ride without her. He and Mistress lead the trail rides."

Her heart quaked, thinking of what would happen to Mistress. She learned to ride on this old mare, and to retire her would be like putting her grandfather out to pasture, too. She blinked back the onset of tears, her throat clogging as she clung to Mistress's halter. The horse shook its head, and Dr. Kingsley patted the horse on the other side of its neck.

"As I said, talk to him. We won't know for sure until I get those X-rays, but Alison, I've seen enough broken legs to know this one won't heal right. She's an old horse. I'm sorry. I know what Mistress means to your grandfather and the Silver Stirrups Riding Club. I wish I had better news. I know that's not the solution you wanted to hear."

"It's not your fault." They'd had a bad streak is all. Last week Alison's mother reminded her that God had everything in His hands, and told her to trust it would come out for the better good. What good could happen for the seniors who came out to ride every week in the Silver Stirrups Riding Club?

Gramps and Mistress had been out riding on that weekly trail ride when Mistress's foot went down into a groundhog hole and tripped. She threw Gramps forward and broke his collarbone. Very little could keep Dwight Vandergraft down, but at seventy-four, his body didn't heal as fast as he wanted to admit.

The news about Mistress would devastate him.

"We've got some horses over at the rescue. Maybe you can find one or two that will work to replace your loss." Josh reached over and slid his hand down Mistress's blaze. Her ears laid back, and Alison didn't blame the mare. She didn't care for that idea either.

"I need to talk to Gramps."

"You can call the clinic and let Jenny know what you all decide. In the meantime, I'll wrap it back up to hold the swelling down."

"I'll stop by the hospital before I head to work. Randy should get here in a few hours. I'll leave a note for him. Is there is anything else we need to do?"

"Keep her in her stall. The wrap will hold a day or two while Dwight decides what to do."

Alison nodded. "We'll have to cancel next week's ride."

"Can't you lead it?" Josh asked. He had moved away, and the loss of his nearness allowed the anxiety to move in.

"Not without a horse." Losing Gus weighed more heavily on her than ever. "All these other horses are claimed by riders. Some of them look forward to riding that particular horse every week, and I can't take that way from them."

"There's a leggy chestnut at the rescue, needs some groceries, but I've taken her a few times, and Cade seems to think she's sound." Josh lifted his ball cap and scratched, then resettled it. "There's Shorty, she's a big pony, but she'd make a good trail horse."

Dr. Kingsley finished wrapping up Mistress's leg. "Sarah is getting ready for the open house on Saturday. You should stop in and see her."

Michael Kingsley's wife, Sarah, ran the Silver Wind Equine Rescue for abused and abandoned horses. She'd been out to the rescue when Gus had gone missing. She'd printed flyers, and Sarah had promised to keep a lookout for him. It had been weeks since she last stopped in to check with Sarah. The police assured her they were doing all they could, but as time passed, they had more pressing matters than a missing horse.

"I'll do that."

"Looking forward to it," Josh said.

She followed the two men out to Dr. Kingsley's truck, cringing when she added up the numbers of what this visit would cost her. Jenny, Silver Wind's Animal Clinic manager, had been kind, even supportive when Alison explained what happened. Gramps would expect Doc Miller to check Mistress.

Gramps had been using Doc Miller forever.

She prayed he would be open to hearing what this new veterinarian thought best for his mistress.

Behind her, Mistress stood in her crossties, her front leg resting and wrapped.

"I'd keep her tied. Don't have her walking too much on that leg," Dr. Kingsley reminded her. In robot mode, she went through the motions, stood and waited while Dr. Kingsley typed some notes on a laptop sitting on the hood of his truck. She interlaced her fingers, and Josh crossed his arms. A scowl on his face, he glanced around.

"Well, I've got horses to feed and clients to visit."

"Ali," Josh said, and she liked the way he said it. Filled with curiosity and a hint of emotion, it made her pause. No one has called her by that old nickname in years.

"It was good to see you again, Josh."

Closing the laptop, Dr. Kingsley said, "We're done here. Ready?"

"Stop by the rescue before Saturday. I'll be waiting." Josh headed to the truck, his eyes lingering on her a little too long. It made her cheeks warm, and her lips yearn for that one time he'd kissed her goodnight after one of their few dates.

She talked to Gramps before about adopting another horse since they had space. None of them would ever replace her Gus. It wouldn't hurt to give them a chance. Wasn't that what the rescue was all about, second chances? Maybe not only for the horses. Josh tipped his hat as he got in the truck.

Clearing her throat, she hated to ask, but Gramps would want to know. "How much is this going to cost?"

Dr. Kingsley put the laptop in his truck, got in, and rolled down his truck window. "We'll work it out, Alison, don't you worry."

But she worried.

She couldn't help it. She had enough troubles to sink the *Titanic* if the ship hadn't already sunk over a century ago.

Back in the barn, she walked up to Mistress and wrapped her arms around the mare's neck. "Gramps isn't about to let go of his mistress. Don't you give up either."

Mistress stood, her front leg extended out to take the pressure off.

"It won't hurt to look at those other horses. They need a home, too. We'll see what Gramps says when I visit him this afternoon. Don't you worry girl, no one will take your stall. Gus will find his way back to us soon."

God willing.

Chapter Two

Josh watched from the side mirror as Alison went back into the barn and disappeared from view.

I'll be waiting.

What kind of desperate remark had that been? Her cheeks had turned a shade pink, and all he could think of was the last time he kissed her on his way out of town. She let her hair grow past her shoulders, and he liked it this way. He itched to reach out and touch a strand to see if it was still as silky-soft as it had been when they were teenagers.

Stop. Right now. Don't think about it.

Too late. He already had, and Josh wouldn't be able to get Alison out of his head for the rest of the day. She could have married by now or have a boyfriend. He had no business of drudging up the past and mulling over it after all this time.

There was something about seeing her after all this time, but since when did he ever consider going back to see a girl a second time? Not since Alison. Not since the summer he went along with his twin, Jenny, to work on the Kingsley Estate as a stable hand. It was the summer life changed for so many of them, and Josh couldn't blame Alison one bit if she didn't come around him again.

Time had a way of softening the heart and allowing room to forgive, but those things overlooked were never forgotten. He never took Alison as the type to hold a grudge, and she seemed to move on fine without him after that summer. It made him think the time they spent together meant more to him than her.

Then why did it bother him so much after all this time?

It's not like he made her any promises. They were dating, and she was sixteen.

Just like Jenny's best friend, Sarah, was sixteen when she got involved with Michael Kingsley. And eventually, Michael and Sarah got their second chance.

Would Alison give him one too?

Down the road aways, Michael said, "You two seemed to know each other."

"We went to school together." And Josh left it there.

Michael seemed to sense he wouldn't get anything more out of him. Glad he didn't press for more information, Josh settled back in the truck seat. He rode along to escape hanging banners with Cade for the horse rescue's open house on Saturday. Once a month, Sarah insisted they hang banners, put out coffee, tea, and cookies for people in hopes those who came would find a horse to adopt.

Alison would come on Saturday. She had to, for the sake of finding a horse, and because he hoped hard, she did. He realized he needed to see her again. He owed her an explanation. He couldn't go on living with himself if he didn't tell her the truth. It might not matter to her. In a lot of ways, it mattered to him. Maybe this is what he needed to move on and find someone like his sister, Jenny, had found the one God had for her when she ran into Cade.

With the farm fields going past in the window at his elbow, Josh wished he could have left it in his mind, the way Alison's doe eyes gazed at him. He always believed her eyes alone could steal a man's soul. So innocent and bright, he loved her enthusiasm and trust in him. She allowed him to dream without having anyone laugh at him. She made him feel like he could tell her anything without judgment.

And then he got all dumbstruck that summer apart, and things happened between Sarah and Michael that made Josh listen to advice from Jenny. As if being born a few minutes before him made her any older or wiser, he scuffed.

Young. Foolish. Love made people do stupid things.

Responsibility called for doing right by others. Life demanded safe and secure paths, which Josh never took. His father never understood why Josh refused to go to college. Someone had to watch out for Sarah. Jenny made him promise. While his sister went off to follow in their father's footsteps with an accounting degree, Josh stayed behind.

Besides, Josh blamed himself for getting Sarah in trouble in the first place.

Not him, exactly. Michael had done a fine job of getting Sarah in the family way, and Josh had done a crappy job of keeping her from getting in that situation in the first place. All those years, he figured he owed it to his sister and her best friend for failing to keep two scheming teenage girls out of trouble. His father sent him that summer to keep his sister from doing anything she shouldn't. Josh figured as a self-appointed brother of his sister's best friend, Sarah had become his responsibility, too.

And he planned to go as far as marrying Sarah to save her from her grandmother's wrath back then, if she would have had him. It crushed his pride more than his heart. He knew her heart belonged to Michael. Josh understood the preservation of one's feelings. He held his own deep in his breast pocket.

Rather than see the hurt in those adoring brown eyes of Alison's, he chose to avoid her and thus avoid the pain he feared he would cause them both. He worked at the auction house and as a farmhand while Alison moved on and went off to college to forget him. That entire last year of high school, he went to a vocational school and went out of his way, along with Jenny, to support Sarah.

Guilt, a hard pill to swallow, punched him in the gut.

But even after all these years, Alison could make a man forget to breathe.

"I think Jenny said we need to stop at Jake Harstead's place to check a bunch of cows."

Josh checked Michael's schedule, grateful for the distraction. "Then, Millers.'"

"I appreciate you coming along to help sling up Campbells' cow."

"You think it has a chance?" Josh rolled back his shoulder, thinking of the big Holstein they ratcheted cables and a sling under to hold up after doing a spread eagle in the barn during the morning dash to the milking pen.

"Pinched nerve, some do recover." Michael shrugged, his hands steering the truck, a grimace on his face. "More so than Vandergrafts' horse. It's a shame. The last thing they needed out here was to lose another horse. I hope Sarah can set Alison up with a horse or two, so the Silver Stirrups program isn't interrupted. I know Sarah's been keeping a lookout for Alison's horse."

"Alison's horse?" A sick feeling slid to the pit of Josh's stomach.

"Someone stole it right out the barn a few months back. I pray she gets it back. Especially with what's happened to Mistress. If I didn't know better, I'd think someone was out to sabotage the Silver Stirrups Riding Club"

Josh leaned back in the seat. "Stolen?"

"Ask Sarah. She'd know more. I'm surprised you didn't know."

"Sarah mentioned a horse going missing." Josh swallowed down the unease building inside him. "I didn't know it was from Windy Knoll."

"Walked it out in the middle of the night. No tracks, so the police think someone rode the horse away or led it up the road to a waiting truck."

"No wonder Alison is upset. I don't get that someone would want to sabotage a riding club for a bunch of seniors."

"And they may not. It could be a streak of bad luck. Lord knows we have all gone through a period of it from time to time."

"My mom always said things happen in threes. Not superstitious, but expecting the next thing seems to lessen the blow, she would say, and remind us to pray."

"I think the Vandergrafts could use a few prayers right now."

"Of all the bad timing." Josh turned his head to look out the window.

"Too late to regret coming out here with me," Michael said.

"It was that or listen to Cade grumble about Jenny wanting to paint the kitchen a second time." Inside the truck cab started to get stuffy. He leaned forward and adjusted the air vent.

Michael chuckled. "You'll learn someday that women need to nest. It's an internal thing they got going on. But I have to say. I'm glad Sarah loves the farmhouse the way her gram left it."

Relieved for the shift in conversation, Josh said, "You wait, Jenny will convince Sarah something needs to be changed, and you'll be moving furniture like last month in Dillon's room."

"Totally my idea. There comes the point when a man needs privacy with his wife." Michael grinned.

Josh didn't need to hear how much privacy. He pointed ahead. "You can turn there. It'll cut a few minutes off the main route."

Michael glanced at the directions on his phone. "Jenny doesn't know all the back roads as I do so you won't find it programmed in your app. Trust me. I know these roads."

"You know where you're going." They turned down the road Josh indicated.

Josh's mind was right back on Alison. Her missing horse. Her grandfather's injured mare.

Alison deserved someone who could give her stability and wildflowers.

At the very least, he could help find her a horse and ensure nothing else kept the Silver Stirrups Riding Club from going out on the trail.

Back at the clinic, Josh walked into the empty waiting room.

Jenny's gaze drifted up at the sound of the bell. "How did it go out at the Vandergrafts'?"

"Alison will call you and let you know what Dwight decides to do." He hated the pained expression on her face at having to relay the diagnosis to her grandfather.

"That bad?" Jenny leaned back in her office chair. His sister's dark red tresses hung in spiked layers against her round cheeks. A gleam of sadness had set in her eyes along with that thin-lipped expression she used around him all too often.

He understood all too well what it was like when a person's luck ran out. Luck wouldn't save Dwight Vandergraft's mare, it might bring back Alison's horse, and all it ever did for Josh was get him deeper in other people's debt. He thought of Jenny's husband, Cade, who got him out of a scrap last year that could have cost him dearly. Thankful, his brother-in-law had kept the incident from reaching Jenny's ears. Otherwise, his goody-two-shoes sister wouldn't have let him forget it.

Some things were better forgotten, and some things were worth holding onto.

And there was only one way to find out.

Josh leaned against the front desk. "Mistress's leg is broken."

"Dwight's horse?" Jenny's jaw dropped. "No. Not Mistress! Doesn't Dwight use that horse to lead the Silver Stirrups trail rides?"

"Yep, that would be the one." Josh scratched his jaw. He would have shaved if he knew he would run into Alison. His finger tapped his jaw, not liking the unsettling feeling he had since leaving Windy Knoll's Stable.

Michael came in, sat the laptop on the desk for Jenny, and disappeared down the hall. "Sarah's waiting for him to go along with her for Dillon's appointment. You all are late, and Sarah's had the baby in the car waiting."

"What do you expect with a dairy with two dozen cows needing pregnancy checked?" Josh shrugged.

Jenny watched and waited for the first sign of a customer coming down the hall from their appointment with Doc Miller. Josh stepped back while Jenny took care of the paperwork, and the woman with the cat took it and left.

Once the bell stopped jingling and the door closed, Jenny rounded on Josh. "Spill."

Of course, his sister wouldn't let it go until she squeezed every detail out of him.

"What? I told you the horse's leg is broke."

His twin had the eyes of a cat, sharp and canny. They narrowed in on him. "I know that look. What aren't you telling me?"

Under Jenny's glare, his skin itched. He knew better than to scratch, or Jenny would see guilt in his action.

"Alison's grandfather is in the hospital."

She punched him in the arm. "I told you that before you went with Michael out there."

Josh moved out of Jenny's reach.

She tilted her head. "Was Alison there?"

"Yeah. I invited her on Saturday." His voice betrayed him, or call it twin instincts because Jenny lifted an eyebrow. He couldn't get anything past her.

"What's that mean? You invited her? Where? On a date?"

Josh glared at her, letting his annoyance show. "She needs a horse, Jen. Two, from what I hear. Where better to help her find one than at the open house? There's at least one I can think of that might work for an intermediate rider. Cade might be able to work with that leggy thoroughbred to make her suit for Dwight."

"Is that the only reason you invited her?" Jenny pulled Michael's laptop closer. She flipped it open, peering over the screen in wait for an answer.

"Can't a man help a girl out without any other motive?"

"This isn't any other girl or one of your random dates."

"It was a long time ago." Josh hated the bitter taste in his mouth. He hated the twist of guilt in his stomach. "She could be married for all I know."

He must have lost his mind for flirting with her.

Jenny pecked at the keys on Michael's laptop, glancing up to say, "Not married. She told Sarah she broke up with her boyfriend a few months ago. Not long after, her horse got stolen."

"And the police haven't found it?"

"And the boyfriend doesn't have it." Jenny lifted a shoulder in indifference. "I suppose I'd look there first, too. You remember Jason Ward?"

"Why would I?"

"He's the guy she hooked up with her last year of high school. He followed her to college and came back here when she did."

"That's a lot of years," he said under his breath. "Talk about commitment."

Jenny slapped the laptop closed. "I wouldn't screw it up this time. The next time she might marry him."

"Who said I'm interested?" Josh's chest tightened. The thought of having Alison look at him with those big doe eyes and giving into falling in love with her all over again made him want to get in his truck and head for higher country. Better now than never, his mother would say. The timing could cost him everything. It had last time.

"Oh, you're interested." Jenny stood, careful of the baby bump she carried. "It's written all over your face, brother. You like her! Don't get me wrong, for a while there I thought you'd end up with Sarah, but God had other plans. And now that Sarah's settled with Michael, you've got no more excuses. You like Alison Vandergraft, and now that you're both available, it scares you to think about tying the knot."

"Geez, Jen. Slow down. I haven't even asked her on a date."

Behind him, the bell sounded, and Cade walked in.

Jenny's lips curved into a smile. "You invited her to the open house on Saturday."

"To help her and Sarah. Win. Win." Josh walked away while he still had the last word. Tipping his hat, he went past Cade, "It's a good thing you showed up. All those baby hormones are going to her head."

Cade chuckled. "Who is she trying to set you up with now?"

"Alison Vandergraft and I ain't setting him up. He invited her to the open house on Saturday." Jenny tilted her head for Cade's kiss.

"I invited a few folks last week. Does that mean I'm in trouble?" Cade appeared perplexed.

Josh laughed. "See what I mean?"

Jenny glared at him, then smiled sweetly up at her husband. "Did you date any of them in high school?"

Cade shook his head.

"Then you got nothing to worry about." She rested her cheek against his shoulder, smiling again, this time at Josh like the cat who caught the canary.

"She's all yours," Josh told Cade, leaving the happy couple to their few moments of alone time.

Chapter Three

First thing Saturday morning, Alison went to visit Gramps. Several members of the Silver Stirrups Riding Club had stopped in to visit him throughout the past few days, bringing flowers to brighten up the sterile room. Meals arrived at the ranch, and between checking on her clients, Alison spent her evenings freezer-packing most of the casseroles. If any more food arrived, she didn't know where she'd put it all. They had enough upside-down cakes and lasagna for a few months with only her and Gramps in the house.

Around ten o'clock, the doctor came in and argued with Gramps, but because Alison would be there to watch over him most of the time, the doctor reluctantly agreed to let Gramps come home.

Gramps wouldn't make any decision about his mistress until he got home to see her.

Alison's heart broke for them both. Grandma passed a few years ago, and Mistress had been the one to help him through that time the most. It was because of Grandma Vandergraft Alison had been inspired to start the Silver Stirrups Riding Club to help Gramps through his mourning.

By two that afternoon, Alison had Gramps settled in his favorite chair with reruns of John Wayne westerns playing on the television. Later, Randy offered to come over to help her take Gramps out to the barn to see Mistress. He would have to take it easy for several weeks until his collarbone and his hip healed from the fall. She made sure he had a tall glass of iced tea and a snack by his recliner.

She decided to wear her hair down, fussing more with a smear of gloss and some color on her cheeks. Every time she glanced in the mirror, she gave herself a little pep talk unsure which made her more nervous — seeing Josh, or potentially replacing one of their precious horses. Not a replacement, an addition, she told herself. Just like she kept reminding herself this wasn't a date. There would be other people there. She was going to see a man about a horse. Her insides squeezed. So what if that man happened to be Josh Anderson. She had to keep her head on straight and focus. Gramps needed her to take care of him. The riding club depended on her support to direct things while Gramps healed.

Her mother would come down from Georgia on Tuesday to visit, and she promised her mother she could take care of the riding club, her job, and Gramps. Staying busy had been the one thing to assist her in getting over the sudden changes in her life. Too many surprises had her heart in a bind and her head in the clouds of late.

Curiosity burned inside her nonetheless. She had no business bringing up the past. It seemed foolish to dwell on it, especially since she dated Jason. She clenched her jaw as she thought about her ex-boyfriend. It seemed like they had been joined at the hip for a big part of her life. They'd dated since high school, and her family always assumed he would be the one she would marry. Jason insisted she was the only girl for him, God's perfect gift to him. But for some reason, her heart could never fully commit when he pressed her to take his ring. She rubbed her bare ring finger on her left hand.

Jason pushed her to move in with him when he got his new place in Shelbyville, even though he knew how she felt about such an arrangement before marriage. She joked there would be no place for Gus, her spirited leopard print Appaloosa. Jason claimed to have an allergy to horses, or maybe it was because Gus never took to him. Her gelding would lay back his ears when Jason came around. Several times when Jason came to the barn to see her, Gus would take a swipe at him with hoof or teeth. Horses had a way of sensing things about people. At first, she assumed Gus didn't like men, but he only did it around Jason.

Her oversized pony had tried to tell her Jason was a bad apple, and she owed her horse an apology. She prayed one day she got the opportunity. She wouldn't ever give up on finding him.

Thinking of Gus, she plopped down on the chair across from Gramps.

"I thought you were going out to the horse rescue this afternoon."

"That was before you came home. It's getting late in the day. I can go out another time."

"You can go out right now. By the looks of you, I'd say there's more than a horse you're trying to impress."

Alison laughed, a habit when she got nervous. "Josh Anderson came by with Dr. Kingsley to see Mistress. He works out at the rescue, and he invited me to come out today."

Gramps grunted. "You be careful. That boy gets around. He's at the auction house some nights, and he hauls for whoever has got cash."

"I move around to different clients every day, Gramps. Not all of us have the privilege of doing one thing to make ends meet." Not sure why she suddenly felt so defensive of a man she hardly knew anymore.

Gramps gave her the eye. It's how he looked when he suspected someone said something with a bit of wisdom to it. "After that last guy, I'd hope you would take your time in picking another. You had enough sense to step away from the other one. I know you'll use the good whit God gave you going forth."

Alison laughed again. "Gramps."

"I suppose we could use another horse. Maddy Pierce hasn't been able to come on the rides since old Star got put out to pasture. Don't suppose Randy is available to go with you. Being Saturday, he's probably playing chess over at Harrison's."

"I'll be fine." She loved that he worried about her. They both knew he wanted Randy to go along because of Josh more so than the horse. Her grandfather still had old-fashioned sentiments about unmarried females going places without someone else along.

"You've got a good eye for finding the good ones. Make sure you find one with a gentle temperament. Maddy isn't an expert rider. There is no harm in looking, Alison. Don't feel obliged to take any of them if they don't suit. We don't need any rotten apples in the barn."

"Yes, Gramps." She tried to hold back a smile she felt forming at at hearing his stern voice.

"I know it's hard, sweetheart, but sometimes we have to make tough choices to move on."

She bent close and kissed his cheek. "I'll do my best."

She had time to think about it on the ride over to the Silver Wind Equine Rescue. A few cars remained, and Alison wondered if she came too late, if all the horses had been adopted. Then she chided herself for such a silly idea. Adopting a horse was a process, not like going and picking out a pooch at the pet store and walking home with it the same day. There would be papers to fill out and an adoption fee, sure. Then a home visit a few weeks later, if she remembered Sarah explaining it right when she'd gone there when Gus had first gone missing.

Driving down the lane past the rescue sign, she bit her lip and stopped. She would mess up her gloss, and she forgot to bring it with her.

She tried to hold down that everlasting spark of hope of one day pulling up to a barn and finding Gus inside. She gave herself a few extra moments after parking to settle those hopes and tuck away the jitters tickling through her belly.

Outside in the ring, a couple with a young girl walked around with a stout little pony.

It distracted Alison enough to pull her from her car and walk close to spy the girl's beaming face as she held onto the lead line.

"Cute."

Alison jumped, surprised at the voice so close behind her.

She whirled around, her hand on her heart, to see the shocked face of Josh. "Josh Anderson, you about scared me half to death sneaking up on a girl like that!"

"Whoa!" Josh put up his hands, a flush of guilt in his face. "I didn't sneak, and I'm sorry you didn't see me."

She let her hand slide away from her heart. "I suppose I could have been a little sidetracked."

"Still cute." He winked.

And she laughed. "Yes, that pony with the little girl is cute."

Josh came closer, leaned his shoulder into hers. "I wasn't talking about them, but I'll agree. Buster and Brittany are getting along really well. I suspect she'll be taking him home by next week to use as a 4-H project until she outgrows him."

Alison watched Brittany tug on the lead and change the direction she took him.

"Hey, why the sad face?"

"I remember my first pony. I hated having to see Butterscotch go when I was too big to ride her, and Scott had a pony of his own. I know

23

my dad and Gramps found her a good home when they got me another bigger one to ride. It's sweet and sad at the same time. You know?"

"Not really." Josh shrugged. "I never had a horse of my own."

Alison's jaw went slack. "Really?"

Josh stuck his hands in his back pockets. "There was always someone else who needed theirs taken care of, or didn't have the time to ride it. Why bother my parents to board one for me when I could be around as many as I wanted whenever I wanted?"

"It's not the same." Alison could see the truth in his eyes that he tried to hide from others. The one thing she always admired about Josh was that he never lied to her. Not that he didn't avoid telling her the truth, but when he opened his mouth, he didn't lie to her, either. She got a glimpse of the little boy who wanted the pony and most likely couldn't have it for circumstances out of his family's control.

"Not that it matters." Josh tilted his head toward the barn. "It's not me you are here looking for a horse for."

Alison smiled, suppressing the laugh bubbling up inside her. "Could be."

She piqued his interest. He left his hat behind this afternoon, and the sunlight danced across his reddish hair. He quirked a brow, those green eyes dancing with anticipation, and it made her heart do a little flip.

"Alison Vandergraft, are you trying to set me up?"

Then she did laugh. Laying her hand on his arm, she batted her lashes and playfully flirted. "Didn't you tell me you had a leggy thoroughbred here?"

Josh grinned from ear to ear. He grabbed her hand and tugged her in the direction of the barn. "Right this way, my lady."

All the nervous energy from earlier seemed to melt away when his hand took hers. It felt like back when they were teenagers, holding hands, stealing kisses. She stopped at thinking about those kisses. Her cheeks a little too warm, she squinted in the dim interior of the stables as Josh weaved her around people in green T-shirts. One of them had a baby in her arms, who Alison recognized as the owner, Sarah. A man stood talking with a woman by a stall as they passed it. Josh slowed down when they went around the corner to the next set of stalls at the end. A dark brown horse stood in a stall munching on hay and kept its face out of reach. "This is Destiny's Calling."

"She's a racehorse."

"She's got great endurance." Josh slid open the stall and reached in to get Destiny's halter.

He talked to the horse. "Don't you, girl?"

"She might be more than what we need for the trail rides. Most of our riders are experienced, but we've got some newcomers who haven't ever ridden before. I'm thinking something not so leggy and a bit more laid back like a quarter horse or Appaloosa."

Josh ran his hand down the horse's blaze. "Sorry, girl, I tried."

Alison held back for reaching in to pat the horse. "Have you ridden her?"

"A few times. She's quiet and sound. She's got endurance, as I said, but not real fast. She spooks at traffic, but you get none of that out on the trail."

She had to hand it to him. He didn't give up. "I think you missed your calling. You should have been a car salesman or, in this case, a horse dealer."

"He is, at that, isn't he?" A man limped closer. He wore a green T-shirt, and Alison recognized him from speaking with the woman when they passed.

Josh slid the stall door shut again. "Alison Vandergraft, this is my brother-in-law, Cade Sheridan."

"Nice to meet you." She shook hands with him. Noticed how when she stepped back, Josh's arm rested above her, holding on to the bars of the stall door.

"You might want to show her old Texas. He came from that lot with the pony and the crippled one the humane society recovered in West Virginia. He's slow and gets a little grumpy when you saddle him, but he'll follow along on the trail. He might be good for a beginner. He'll work well for someone who knows a little bit about how to stay in the saddle."

"What he's saying is you'll have to keep giving ole Texas a swift kick once in a while to keep him going."

"Perfect." Alison clapped her hands together. "I'd love to meet him."

Cade hitched his thumb. "He's out in the arena. The woman I was speaking to had him out for a ride. He's a bit shy on weight. You'll want to increase his feed gradually, and he gets as much grass as a horse can eat out in the pasture rotation with the others."

"He gets along with others?" Alison asked.

"Some don't like him, but he doesn't cause no trouble. Come on. I'll introduce you." Josh put his arm around her, steered her away from Cade.

She glanced back at the cowboy and waved. "Thanks."

Ole Texas stood with one back hoof resting as he snoozed. "Oh, you and Maddy Pierce might be the perfect match."

"Maddy Pierce?" Josh asked.

Alison walked up to the front of the snoozing horse. She talked as she approached not to spook the gelding. "The woman who would be riding him. Gramps has been looking to get another horse as we don't have enough for everyone wanting to ride. We've talked about doing two rides a week and splitting the group as not everyone owns a horse, and we don't want anyone in the program not to get to participate or feel left out. Gramps has mentioned adding on to the barn or building a smaller one for boarding horses for the club members."

"So, this horse would be for a member and not for your grandfather."

"I'm sure if Maddy could afford it, she'd board a horse of her own, but this way we'd have another horse for anyone who needed it. Which is why it's really important that the horse is friendly, reliable, and can keep up on the trail."

Josh had a bewildered look on his face.

"Some of those senior citizens can ride better than I can," Alison whispered to the horse.

Josh ran his hand down Texas's neck. "You want to take him for a ride? The open house is ending at four p.m., but I don't think Cade or Sarah would mind if I saddled up Destiny and we went for a short ride."

"Oh." Alison stepped back from Texas. The horse bobbed its head as if it understood and agreed. She hadn't ridden since Gus went missing. Sitting atop another horse didn't feel right. Alison pressed her lips together, trying to decide.

Josh tightened the girth. Her silence to him must have meant a yes. He flipped the reins over the horse's neck. "It'll take me a few minutes to get Destiny ready if you want to ride around the ring a few times to get a feel for how he rides."

"Um." Alison tried to figure out a way to decline gracefully. "Isn't he tired from other people riding him today?"

"He's only been out this once. We won't go far, and we'll walk most of the way unless you want to race."

He teased, and that sinful grin of his returned to his face.

She almost kicked herself for wanting to give in. Texas looked at her with big dark eyes that tugged at her heart. He was the right height for a quarter horse, not as tall as Mistress, but about the same size as her Gus. She could see the outline of his ribs, and it would take a few months of grazing and grain to build up his weight and regular exercise to gain more muscle.

Maybe if someone had the time to ride him every day, he'd be able to go on the weekly trail rides. Maddy Pierce could come to ride him. She might have the time. Or Alison, but — Alison wouldn't let her thoughts finish. She shook her head. "I can't."

Josh looked at her, and she felt compelled to explain. "I haven't ridden another horse since Gus. I can't. It feels wrong. I'm sorry. I'm sure Texas is great to ride. I'd like to have Maddy come over and ride him, seeing she'll be the main one taking him out most times. Maybe Randy can come out with her, he's Gramps's friend and helps with the other Silver Stirrups horses."

She turned and walked away, and the look of disappointment in Josh's eyes and all the horses in the stables standing in their stalls caused the uneasy feeling of the walls closing in on her. She lengthened her stride, rushing without running. "I should go. I left Gramps at home. I'll catch you later."

Once she got out of the stables, she didn't bother looking back. She slid into her car, her heart pounding and her chest about to cave in. Through her windshield, she could see the little girl with the black pony. The father stood with rescue owner Sarah filling out papers on a clipboard.

At least somebody was going home with a pony that day.

Chapter Four

Of all the impulsive things Josh had ever done, this had to be among the most idiotic of all, but he'd go with it.

Alison hadn't called or come around the rescue in days. Never one for having much patience, Josh decided to take matters into his own hands. He talked Cade into keeping Jenny out of his hair and distracted while he informed Sarah of his decision shortly after supper. He didn't have many daylight hours left, and he wasn't one for going back and changing his mind.

Sarah appeared more amused at him than irritated with him as he told her what he had planned. Of course, ole Texas didn't seem to mind.

"Can't figure out what I said to make her leave," Josh confessed to Sarah.

Swaying with little Dillon on her hip as he whined, needing his afternoon nap, Sarah said, "I don't think it's you."

She pulled Dillon up so his head could rest on her shoulder. "I can appreciate what she might be feeling. She probably feels awkward riding another horse. While Gram might have sold mine, it's different from having someone steal it without evening knowing who or why and being worried about getting it back."

Josh scratched his chin with his index finger as he paused outside the doorway to the barn. Maybe this was a bad idea coming here, though bringing her the horse had been a good excuse. He couldn't help wondering what he'd said or done to make Alison so uncomfortable that she'd rush to leave. He ran his hand down ole Texas's neck and said, "Don't take it personally." And even though the horse relaxed and went back to snoozing, Josh couldn't let it go.

After a few days, it seemed to gnaw at him. He even had succumbed to Jenny's request and went to church on Sunday. A part of him hoped he'd see Alison, but he remembered she attended a different church across town.

Muttering a prayer that he wouldn't make a fool of himself or upset Alison again, he walked in the barn. "Hello. Anyone here?"

A man's voice called back, "Back here."

Josh followed the voice and found an older gentleman cleaning out a stall in the back row of the stables. His dark hair had a touch of silver at the temples. Resting on his pitchfork, the man asked, "What can I do for you?"

"I'm looking for Alison. Is she around here?"

The man nodded, looking him up and down as if taking his measure. "She'll be out soon. Probably finishing up supper with Dwight. You need something?"

"I've got a horse for her." Josh held the man's steady gaze, wondering why the man looked at him with such suspicion. "Actually, it's a surprise. She came by the rescue on Saturday and said she'd be back. I guess she must have got busy, but I brought her a horse I think might work for one of the members of the riding club to try out."

"That's awful nice of you." The man grinned, and Josh relaxed. "She'll be out in a few minutes, I reckon." He held Josh's gaze. "I suppose Dwight won't mind since it's horse business."

Josh nodded. The man wasn't Alison's father, as Josh had met the man many times in the past. Whoever this guy was, he seemed to be protective over Alison. It made him feel better to know someone else worried about Alison's well-being.

"I'll wait for her out by my truck."

"If she wants to keep the horse, you can put it in here."

Back out by his truck, Josh shoved his hands in his pockets, pacing alongside the trailer. He should walk up to the house and knock on the door, but the man said Alison would come shortly.

Josh's heart skipped at the sound of her calling his name. "Josh? What are you doing here?"

Oh, you've got it bad, Josh thought with a shake of his head. Was she happy to see him? He gave her his most brilliant smile and walked to meet her. All the scenarios of what he would say flew right out of his brain and left him stumbling for words.

She looked pretty in the tan Carhart jacket, and her blonde hair pulled up in a twist with several strands framing her face. Her pants were stained and ripped in two places. He couldn't have found her more attractive, as he did back when they were in high school.

As she approached, her smile was hesitant, as if she wasn't sure why he was there.

Truthfully, neither did Josh. He pulled his hands from his pockets, then shoved them back in, not sure what to do with them. "The guy inside said you'd be coming out, so I thought I'd wait here. I didn't want to disturb your grandfather if he was resting."

Because you just happened to be in the area and had Texas in the back of your trailer. Get real Josh, she can see right through you, he berated himself. She'll want you to sweep her off her feet for sure now.

Alison broadened her smile. "Gramps is watching another one of his old westerns. You would have been welcome to come in. Is Randy still out here cleaning stalls?"

"Yeah, he's still in there. I could lend a hand if you need help. It seems late to be still cleaning stalls," he offered, not liking the look of concern on her face.

"I know it's warm enough for them to stay outside all night, but after what happened to Gus …" She tried to shrug to hide the hurt that passed over her eyes. "Gramps thinks it's best to keep the horses locked up at night."

"Understood." Josh hadn't been able to put Alison or her missing horse from of his mind. Who would want to steal an old trail horse? He'd spoken to Sarah about it, and it baffled him. Alison's horse was a gelding, and while he had papers, he couldn't have been worth anything enough for someone to want to steal a thousand-pound animal out of the barn. Cattle maybe, but not a horse.

"Especially since I brought you another."

He puzzled her, and her expression mirrored what she did to him inside.

"You've got a horse in there?"

"Ole Texas." Josh walked around the back of the trailer. "You never came back like you said you would, and he got lonely." Okay, half the truth, but Josh would go with it. He let the trailer door swing open and stepped up inside. Texas turned his head and looked at them.

Alison stood at the back of the trailer as Josh untied Texas to turn him around and bring him out. "You shouldn't have done that."

"Of course I should." Inside his head, he could hear Jenny saying, I told you so. "Consider it a trial. Ole Texas needs a place to call home, and you have a rider without a horse."

"Several," she said quietly. "I'm sorry, I haven't made it back to the rescue this week. Things have been kind of hectic around here with Gramps laid up. I have had three additional clients on my schedule this week due to vacations, and Randy's been trying to help keep up here at the barn. He doesn't function well in the cold, so that's why he comes late in the mornings and early in the evenings. Mostly to let the horses out and bring them in, but with my workload and Gramps, I've gotten behind."

"Then, I came in time." Josh led Texas off the trailer and halted him in front of Alison. Lord, did she smell as nice as she looked. He could breathe in the scent of her lavender and fresh-cut grass for a lifetime.

"It's kind of you to bring Texas over. I know Maddy will be thrilled when she comes tomorrow. I think we have space in one of the back stalls. Two of our regular boarders moved their horses after they heard what happened."

Josh resisted pulling her in his arms. He wanted to comfort her in a bad way. "Their loss. I'm sure they'll see that and come back. Not like anyone else in the entire state has a program like Silver Stirrups for the retired community."

Alison's eyes softened as she brought her fingers up to her lips. "Shh … you don't want to say that too loud. Gramps hears you, and we'll both be in trouble."

"What'd I say?"

She laughed and led the way into the barn. "There is no such thing as a retired cowboy."

"Ain't that the truth." Randy walked out from around the row of stalls. "I've got all of them done except for the two in the far back. Maybe this young fellow can help you finish up and bring the horses in for the night. I promised Daisy I'd take her for a walk tonight, and I'm about out of energy for anything more than a short stroll."

Alison walked over and hugged Randy.

Josh patted Texas's head as the horse gave him a bump in the back when he stopped walking.

"Thank you, Randy. I appreciate everything you do. I'll try to keep up better next week," she told him softly.

"You find someone to lead the ride yet?" Randy asked.

Alison shook her head. "I asked Jack Wonner, but his hip is acting up again, but he offered for me to use Diablo."

"Diablo?" Josh couldn't help jumping in the conversation.

"He's much sweeter than his name implies, I assure you," Alison said.

Randy jerked his chin toward ole Texas. "What are you going to do with that one?"

"Oh," Alison glanced over her shoulder at Josh and Texas. "This is Texas. Josh Anderson, this is Gramps's friend Randy, who helps us. But I guess you could figure that out by now." She went a little pink in the cheeks. She turned oblivious of the way Randy's lips thinned, and he crossed his arms. "Josh brought Texas over from the rescue to see if he'll make a good match for Maddy."

"Nobody will get to ride if you don't have a trail master tomorrow. You know those trails as well as your granddaddy, Alison. You should be the one leading the way. You started this program."

"I know, but without Gus — I'm not ready. I can't." Alison bit her lip, glancing between Texas and Josh.

He could see what she was thinking, and he shook his head. He would have to find a way to help Alison get back on a horse again, even if it wasn't her own. "I have cattle to haul down to Waddy and a horse to deliver near Frankfort." And dash it all, by the crestfallen look on Alison's face, if word got around he couldn't deliver he'd be out of business.

He glanced over at Texas shaking his mane and sighed. "What time's this ride?"

"Morning. About ten o'clock," Randy said.

"I suppose I could take the horse since it's at the clinic and deliver it early, then be back for the ride. I have to be in Waddy by three."

Alison's face lit up. "Oh, you will be. It's a short ride, about an hour. We've been lucky with the weather being mild this time of year for February, but some can't deal with being out in the weather for long."

Josh glanced at Randy, standing behind her. His eyes narrowed on Josh.

"You can bring that leggy thoroughbred to ride if you want," she teased him.

"I don't know the way," Josh said, his eyes meeting Randy's hard stare. "You'd have to go with me and show me the way."

"It's marked. All the trails on the ranch are marked for navigating them," Alison said.

Randy cleared his throat. "I'll let you two figure this out. I need to get home, or Daisy will raise a ruckus."

Josh nodded, acknowledging the odd warning in the man's eyes. Too protective, maybe. Then again, he might have heard of Josh's reputation with the ladies. A big fat zero. Texas gave him another bump and started ahead without him.

"I think this guy wants to see his new place."

"Josh."

"Alison." He could play this game with her all day and knew he would lose. "I'll make you a deal." He hadn't made a good bargain in a long while, and he itched to please a certain blonde-haired gal with sadness in her hazel eyes.

"What kind of deal?" she asked, her voice soft and cautious.

He put Texas in the stall Randy had indicated earlier and swung the half door shut. He leaned against it as she slid the latch through to lock it.

"I'll be your trail master tomorrow if you go out on a date with me Friday night."

She glanced at him, surprised by his request. A slow smile made its way to her eyes, and she said, "Only if you like takeout here in the barn at midnight. I have evening duty with Mrs. Crawford until eight, and then I've got Gramps to check on. Besides, I'll have to finish whatever chores are left here at the barn."

Josh tipped up his cap. "I see how you are. Fine. I'll do better than that." He hoped she could pick up on his playfulness. "What do you say," he tapped his chin for effect, "I come and help Randy Friday, and we spend the day together Saturday?"

Texas turned in the stall, sniffing out the new sawdust and getting a feel for his new stall. His head jerked up and snorted.

"I can't. I have three clients on Saturday, too. How about you pick me up for church Sunday, and then we can go for lunch at McKinley's Deli?"

"I don't know." Josh had made a deal with his brother-in-law last year about going to church. After a few months, he started to look forward to the sermons and the people. He never agreed to always go to the same church as his family to hear God's Word, and maybe not having to sit between Jenny and his mother every once in a while wouldn't be a bad idea.

Josh held out his hand. "Sure. Why not? You've got a deal."

She stared at him.

"Take it or leave it before I change my mind." He winked.

Alison laughed. "Why do I feel like I'm getting the better end of this bargain?"

She took his hand, and Josh lifted it to his lips. "Because not only I am going to be your trail master, Alison Vandergraft, I'm also going to help you find your horse."

Josh hurried to kiss her hand. He couldn't believe he let that blurt out.

When he dared glance at her, those hazel eyes looked back wide with shock.

"You'd do that?" her voice so soft and filled with unbelief. "How?"

To the moon and back, Josh realized he done it again, way to soon too admit his feelings and scare her. Or risk a rejection he deserved.

"First things first. I'll finish these stalls, and then I'll give you a hand bringing in the horses."

She sprang on her toes and planted a kiss on his cheek. "Thank you."

Josh felt his face get hot and put on a goofy grin.

Chapter Five

Alison had trouble sleeping all that night. Josh stayed late and apologized more than once that he couldn't come earlier to help in the barn. He told her how he worked at the clinic, hauled livestock for his own business, and worked at the auction house on Thursday nights. All the while, helping with the horse rescue over at Silver Wind, where he lived in the carriage house by the creek. They talked and worked alongside each other as if they'd never been apart.

She sighed.

She completely understood trying to juggle so many things at once. He laughed and shrugged when she asked Josh how he could keep up with so much.

Alison got up early to help Gramps and make him a hot breakfast. Some things never changed, like waking up with the sunrise. She took her coffee and sat at the little nook by the window in the kitchen. After reading her morning devotions and saying a prayer for Gramps, Gus, and even her ex-boyfriend Jason, she set out to visit her first client.

Once she arrived, it didn't take her long to get Mrs. Crawford up for the morning, dressed, and a cup of steaming coffee by the woman's favorite chair. Alison made sure the older woman took her medication and had a snack for later. On other days, she'd sit and visit for a while in the high-back chair on the other side of the little end table between them. This morning she needed to get back to the ranch before the others came to prepare for their weekly trail ride.

Alison moved the bag of yarn within reach of Mrs. Crawford. While she walked across the cozy little living room to gather up a crocheted afghan Mrs. Crawford favored to warm her lap, the older woman said, "Don't you fuss over me now. I know you got other places you got to get this morning."

Never one to admit she needed more than Alison's company, Mrs. Crawford picked up the yarn and hook and settled them on her lap. "Them horses can't saddle themselves."

Alison draped the blanket at the back of Mrs. Crawford's chair. "It's warm today. The sun will be out, but it's still going to be in the high forties today. You might need this. Is Gail coming by for lunch?"

Mrs. Crawford wiggled in her chair to make herself more comfortable and leaned back. "Didn't say she wasn't."

Alison had to smile. She knew how much Mrs. Crawford looked forward to when her daughter slipped away from her job at the insurance agency down the street to bring her lunch.

"Good. Maybe she'll bring you some of that cheddar broccoli soup that you love."

Mrs. Crawford made a noise in her throat, but her eyes sparkled, letting out she most likely had been thinking the same thing. "Don't you forget about Mozart."

"Of course not." Alison patted Mrs. Crawford on the shoulder and went inside her small kitchen. Mozart, Mrs. Crawford's beloved gray and black striped cat, stood at his bowl, lapping up a bit of milk in his breakfast bowl. Alison hunched down and ran her hand over the cat's head and back. Mozart arched, and a contented purr vibrated through his body. "No knocking things over while I'm gone."

Last week, Mozart had taken to the window sill in the living room and knocked over two of Mrs. Crawford's spider plants. When she came, she found Mrs. Crawford on the floor, trying to clean it up and had to help her on her feet again. She made plant hangers with some baler twine out in the barn and hung them for Mrs. Crawford so Mozart couldn't make a mess again.

The cat blinked at her, and Alison gave him one last stroke down his back. "I'll be back later."

She went back in to see if Mrs. Crawford needed her to do anything else before she left, and the answer had been no. "You go on now. Have a good time on that ride. I'll see you later this evening."

"I won't be riding," Alison said.

Mrs. Crawford clucked her tongue. "If a bunch of over-the-hill folk like me can get their rumps up in the saddle, I don't see what a young person like you can't."

She tried to imagine Mrs. Crawford up in the saddle of a horse. Not a petite lady, but diabetes had weakened the muscles in the older woman's legs, and at eighty-six, Mrs. Crawford carried more spunk than physical energy. She couldn't see as well as she once did, so she liked to listen to the television and crochet until her hands got tired. Then she would take a nap, and when Gail arrived, she'd have lunch and nap again for a little in the afternoon.

"One of these days, I'm going to get you out in that barn and hitch up the surrey. I'll take you for a ride."

Mrs. Crawford smiled. "That's what you say. I'm not that old that I can't travel by motor vehicle."

The older woman's humor warmed her as Alison grabbed her scarf and jacket. "One of these days."

Mrs. Crawford grinned. Mozart came out from the kitchen and hopped up on her lap. As Alison said her goodbye and stepped out onto the porch, she halted at the stairs. Jason's sport utility vehicle sat parked along the sidewalk.

Hitching up the strap of her bag, Alison walked carefully down the frozen stairs of Mrs. Crawford's house. There wasn't much snow with the warm spell they'd been having, and the sidewalk was coated with a sheen of ice from the melting snow freezing in the night.

Concentrating on her steps, she tried to focus on them and not her ex-boyfriend getting out of his vehicle.

"Alison. Let me help you. It's slippery." He took long strides to reach her.

"What are you doing here?" She didn't mean to make it blunt and to the point. Weeks had passed since Gus had gone missing, and Jason had come around offering his sympathy. He wanted her back, asked her to come back, and they'd find Gus together. It wouldn't have been fair to him or even Gus, as her heart belonged more to missing her horse than Jason.

"I heard about Gramps and wanted to help. I've got the day off. I was gonna head out to the ranch, but I knew you'd be here first this morning."

Her routine hadn't changed much in the past few months. Mrs. Crawford had been her client for almost a year now.

"That's kind of you, but we're fine." She bit her tongue at saying more, a part of her feeling bad for not wanting Jason to come by or help. God forgive her for taking away any blessing he might have been, but a bigger part of her wanted to move on and wanted him to move on. Knowing Jason, he would see this as an invitation back in her life. She had no intention of misleading him or allowing him to push her back into a place she never wanted to be in again.

"You canceled the ride today, right? I mean, isn't a little cold for having a bunch of elderly people out on horses anyway?"

"Cold for whom? The horses are used to the weather, and as long as they don't get lathered up, a walk through the woods and clean, brisk air will do both horse and rider some good." She didn't know why she always felt she needed to explain things to him because Jason didn't know much about horses, not like Josh.

She looked at her watch. "I should get going."

Jason shuffled from one foot to another, his leather shoes polished without a scratch. Did he think to wear those to the barn?

"I'll follow you. You can let me know when we get there what I can do to help."

Alison didn't want to be rude. "What about your allergies?"

Jason shrugged. "I took medication this morning. I should be good for the day."

He never said that before or cared to come to the barn. A bunch of sirens welled in her head, warning this was another one of his manipulative attempts to rein her back in his arms.

"I'm sorry, Jason. I appreciate your offering to help, but there isn't much for you to do." Then an idea popped in her head. Was it wrong to test a man's intentions? "Although there is something."

"Sure thing. Name it." He looked eager to please her, his eyes glistening and genuine. She learned a long time ago that those eyes held a great multitude of falsehoods.

"The stalls need to be clean every day, and we're getting short on hay down in the feed room. I could use a hand there."

Jason's face wrinkled up. "You want me to clean stalls? Don't you turn the horses out?"

And that is precisely what she expected him to say. Alison crossed her arms to block the icy breeze. "They're not dogs, Jason. They have to have their stalls cleaned every day."

"Why don't you ask your new stable boy to do it?"

She detected a bit of jealousy in his voice. "I don't know what you're talking about. Randy has always helped at the farm, and he's doing the best he can."

"I'm not talking about Randy." Jason appeared smug. "You know, the word is he's not reliable. He doesn't stick to one thing for long."

"Randy?" She grew tired of playing games, one of the reasons she would never have a future with him. She thought of Josh, of seeing him soon, but Jason's response unsettled her.

"Anderson. Seriously, Alison? If you need someone, you should have come to me. I will always be here for you. No matter what." He stepped toward her, took her arms in his hands. "Why didn't you call me?"

"Like I called you when Gus went missing?" Alison shook her head. "I told you, Jason. We can't be friends. We can't be anything. Please, stay away from me and the ranch."

She turned and hurried to her car. Without hesitation, she started the engine. Despite the cold, she couldn't afford to allow the interior to warm up. Even with the heater on, the chill seeping deep into her bones wouldn't pass until she made sure to put distance between them.

As she headed back to the ranch, relief spread through her as she saw he wasn't following her.

43

By the time she got back, several members of the Silver Stirrups Riding Club had arrived. Dorothy, Clint, and Ed mingled in the barn. Dorothy hummed as she brushed down Trooper in anticipation of the ride. Someone made coffee. Alison could smell it from the old storage room she had turned into a lounge despites Gramps's protests. Clint had a muffin, and Alison wondered if his wife had packed banana or blueberry this week.

Seeing them in the barn, the horses getting prepped and ready for the ride, lifted her spirits. Down on the end of the first row, Mistress whined. Alison greeted everyone. She made her way down to Mistress's stall. "No one has forgotten you, girl."

She reached in and patted the side of the mare's face. Gramps promised he would come out later today to see his mistress. She could tell he was putting if off and couldn't blame him. For Mistress's sake, the clinic had called, and a decision needed to be made soon. While Alison and Randy kept Mistress comfortable in her stall, she prayed the misery for both Gramps and his horse would bring peace for both of them.

"Randy told us about Mistress." Dorothy came up alongside Alison. "Some of us thought we'd stop up at the house after the ride and visit with Dwight if you think that is okay. We've been praying for him and this one." Dorothy put her hand out toward Mistress. The mare shied away.

"I think that is a great idea. Gramps would like to see you all. And I know he appreciates the prayers. I'm afraid he is going to have trouble making the right decision."

"No one ever wants to say goodbye."

Alison felt herself starting to tear up. "At least he'll get the opportunity."

Dorothy hugged her. "Perhaps it is meant to be that way. If you don't ever say goodbye, then perhaps it's not forever."

Alison nodded. "It's all in God's will. I hope I see Gus again."

"You will," Dorothy, a mother of four and grandmother of ten, assured her at the front of the stable as Maddy Peirce walked in. The older woman's hair hid under her knit hat. Her husband, Bob, stood behind her. A whole foot taller than his wife, Bob and Maddy made an interesting pair. "I told her I could toss her up behind me for the ride," Bob said.

"I don't think that will be necessary."

Dorothy called a greeting, and they walked together to receive hugs. "I heard we have a new horse in the barn and possibly a new trail master." Dorothy wiggled her brows toward Alison.

No doubt, Randy had been making phone calls while walking Daisy last night. It made her wonder who and how many others he felt compelled to call and discuss the club matters with.

He hadn't told Maddy or Bob, because Maddy's face went from scowling at her husband to surprised. "A new horse?"

"His name is Texas." Alison wouldn't stay mad at Randy for long. He had good intentions, and he probably figured his telling others was a contribution, not a sin. One thing bothered her, though, about Jason knowing about Josh. He could have only found out from Randy.

"I can't wait to meet him," Maddy said.

"He's right around here. I am not sure if it's a good idea to take him out today, but maybe you can ride him in the indoor arena for a bit. He still needs a bit of TLC." Alison started to motion for Maddy to follow when she heard the rumbling of a diesel engine truck pulling in. Checking her watch, she grinned. It was fifteen minutes of ten, and he warned her might come late. A burst of joy added to her smile, and

Dorothy glanced past Maddy to the closed door. "Is that our trail master arriving?"

"I assume so. If you ladies excuse me, I'll go check."

Maddy clasped her hands together. "We'll be saying hello to Texas."

The two women moved off, murmurs floating in their wake.

Alison hurried past as Clint raised his steaming cup of coffee. "You saddled up?"

"Waiting for the trail master." Clint grunted, and Bob shook his head.

"You two!" She hurried outside to greet Josh, and right behind him, a sport utility vehicle drove up the lane toward the house. All the joy she held at that moment turned to an awkward sense of foreboding.

Josh grinned at her, slapped the side of his trailer with his hand. "I hope you don't mind. I brought Destiny with me."

"What are you up to?" she muttered, torn between marching up to the house and staying close to Josh. One confrontation with Jason for the day had been enough. She grimaced, thinking she had nothing else to say to him and feeling bad for Gramps.

"I'm not trying to force another horse on you if that's what you're asking. I figured Destiny could use a good stretch of her legs and get some more rider experience in."

"I didn't mean you." Alison watched as Jason got out of the vehicle. He glanced her way and jerked his chin, acknowledging her eyes on him.

Josh followed her gaze. "He's not one of your club members?"

"Whatever gave you that idea?" She tried to joke, but the seriousness of her tone made it fall short.

Josh stood close beside her, so close her scarf end blew up with the breeze and slapped his chest.

"Is something wrong?"

Alison shook her head. She wouldn't let Jason ruin this for her, for everyone. She started walking toward the house. "Nothing I haven't already taken care of. I need to check on Gramps while you all get the horses ready."

Josh matched her footsteps. "I think I'll come with you if you don't mind. It looks like your grandfather has company."

"None he'd open the door for." And she assessed correctly, as Jason stood to knock. After a while, he turned and started back to his vehicle. Halfway to the house, Jason got into his car and turned around, heading back down the lane. He slowed as he came closer to Alison and Josh, his gaze on her instead of the road. He came to almost a stop and rolled down his window. "Stopped to see Gramps."

Josh stepped closer to her, his arm went around her, and she leaned into him for support. "He's probably resting."

"I'll come back around supper, bring some takeout from that little dive you like so much."

Alison put on her best smile, let her arm go around Josh's waist, and called, "No need." Her voice trembled. Without Josh's arms holding her steady she might not have had the strength to stand up to him again. Everything in her body started to shake a little.

"We've got plans tonight — the whole family."

Alison glanced up at Josh and whispered, "We do?"

Josh grinned at her, then glanced back at Jason's scowling face. "Maybe another time."

"Thanks for stopping in," she blurted and turned, wanting to run to the barn, but Josh caught her from running. He tipped his head down and pulled her close. His lips on her cold cheek shocked her, but he kept her close, nuzzled her neck. As she started to relax, Jason's vehicle sped down the lane. Only then did Josh release her. Those mischievous green eyes of his filled with concern. "Ex-boyfriend?"

"How did you know?"

Josh kept his arm around her and steered her toward the trailer where Clint and Bob had led their horses outside. She wondered how long they stood out there.

"I've got a lot of girls who are friends, and sometimes it takes another guy stepping in for the ex to back off."

"Thank you."

Josh tipped his hat. "Anything for my lady."

Her heart did a little flip, even if he'd said it using his best John Wayne impersonation.

"I mean it. Thank you."

"I'm guessing you're not going on the ride with us," Josh said, his face getting a bit red, and she had a feeling it was more from her than the cold.

"I need to check on Gramps. You're welcome to join us for lunch when you're done. I have to run out to check on a client at one."

"You still owe me that date."

"I know."

Josh went around to open the trailer. Relieved, he hadn't pushed her to ride another horse or go on the ride. Suddenly, she remembered to tell him. "Stick to the blue marks on the trees. If it gets too muddy, take the green."

"Yes, ma'am."

It sent a tickle to her ribs and had her giggling and blushing as she headed for the house. *Keep it up, Alison, and you're going to find yourself getting attached to that one again.*

Chapter Six

On Thursday night, Josh worked at the livestock auction. With the unpredictable weather, one day the sun came out and melted the snow, and the next the temperatures dropped so low a man didn't know if he needed a jacket or a snowsuit. Tonight, the wind could freeze a man in place, which wasn't suitable for coming out on sale night. A handful of cattle buyers and locals sat in the warm section of the auction house. Electric heaters ran while those who worked stood by the pens in the back, stomping their feet to keep them from freezing.

Josh came in after the calves went through to grab a hot cup of coffee. He would trade off and let Sean do the same when the older heifers came out. It would be an early night for everyone. He ducked in the office, saw Jean typing everything in the computer, and leaned over the counter to watch her. "What are you doing?"

Her eyes never left the computer screen.

After going out on the trail with the Silver Stirrups Riding Club and having lunch with Alison and her grandfather, he decided he had to make good on his word. He was determined to get Alison reunited with her horse and back in the saddle by spring. He wanted to take her on a long ride and maybe a picnic when the weather decided to turn nice and stay warm for more than a day or two.

"You got records of the last horse sales these past few months?"

That got Jean's attention. She glanced up above her bifocals at him. "You get yourself in a bad horse deal again? Because I warned you after the last time not to be a fool."

Josh rested his elbows on the counter. "It's for a friend. You remember seeing any white horses with brown spots come through here in the last few months?"

Jean rose her eyebrow at him. "We get a lot of horses on the third Saturday of the month. You expect me to pay attention to them?"

"You'd remember this one. You don't see a white Appaloosa with brown spots like a Dalmatian dog often, do you?" Josh tried to describe the horse's unique color pattern in a way Jean might reference. On the wall beside her, pictures of cute dogs and horses decorated her workspace.

She pushed her lips out in thought. Her fingers moved randomly over the keyboard. "Within the last few months?"

"Yep."

"You know who might have brought it in?"

"Nope."

"You got anything other than a description? Papers? A registration name?"

Josh took a sip of his coffee, letting the hot liquid seep in his cold veins. At least his brain hadn't gotten frozen. "Gus."

"Is that the name of the person or the horse?"

"Horse."

"Is that a registration name? 'Cause if it is, you're missing parts of it."

Usually, animal registration names included their farm name, dame, or sire in with the long-winded titles. He reached in his pocket and pulled out his cell phone, about to call Alison and ask. He wondered if she would be with a client and if she was allowed to talk. He hadn't called her before now, and he wasn't sure what to say to her: "Hey, Ali, it's Josh. I'm trying to find your horse as I promised, but I don't think you ever told me its full name." He shook his head and decided to text instead.

This is Josh.

He could see her rolling her eyes at him. No, that would be his sister Jenny. But she'd trusted him with her phone number and he wanted her to know he respected her. He had a sense she didn't give her number out to just anyone.

Thinking about you. Did you say your horse's name was Gus?

He hated to get her hopes up when he didn't even have the name right to search.

"I texted her."

Jean relaxed her fingers. She moved to the mouse and scrolled, glancing at him every few seconds in wait.

Yes.

Is he registered?

Yes

Full name?

Almost a full minute went past.

And then another.

And another.

You there?

Yes. Why?

?

Why do you want his name?

"Why does it matter?" he muttered as he thumbed the letters to text her.

I am asking a friend to see if he came through the auction house.
Gus's reg name is: Gust of Wind
Need I ask why?
LOL. I didn't name him. At least not on paper.
Thanks. I'll let you know if I got any info.
You're the best.

Josh slid the phone back in his pocket. "Gust of Wind."

"I can check in between recording this stuff, but just scanning, I don't see anything. It would be more helpful with the name of who brought it in."

"That's it. I don't know. The horse was stolen a couple of months back."

Jean tilted her glasses down.

"I didn't have anything to do with it." He could imagine the idea she had in her head by the look she gave him.

Jean got up and went to the back of the office where the sales slips came up from the auctioneer. He waited while she grabbed the new handful and came back. Faintly he could hear the rambling of a heifer being auctioned off and had to go.

"Have you checked the security cameras?"

"Jean, I could kiss you!"

"My husband might have something to say about that." She winked. "You can view them down in the check-in area. Tell Charlie to call up if he needs to verify I gave you permission. We'd only have the last three months."

"That's all I need." Josh took his coffee and headed out of the office. "Thanks, Jean!"

"Stay out of trouble, you hear?"

"Trying." And God knew he tried. He learned his lesson from trying to gamble his way out of working and diving into risky investments hoping they'd paid off. He struggled with book learning, and he couldn't sit still in school long enough to pay attention most of the time.

He moved through the auction house, in the back with the pens, and helped sort and move the cattle and the stray sheep that came through for the night.

Several times his mind wandered to Alison. He would text and ask what she was doing, and she'd come back with a reply of *playing with Mozart* or *string puzzles.* She asked him about Gus, and he texted, *looking into it.*

As the auction wrapped up around ten o'clock at night, Josh stayed after. Charlie checked with Jean and left him with the last of the hot coffee and video surveillance tapes for the company. He sat in the old peeling vinyl seat in the check-in station, a small heater at his feet, and slowly fast-forwarded through the footage.

Around two in the morning, his eyes couldn't stay open, and he'd run out of coffee. He let last month's video run, rubbed his eyes, and blinked as the image of a white horse walked up the loading station and looked right into the camera.

White. No spots. Josh resigned to calling it a night.

On Sunday, Josh traded his favored tattered old Slugger ball cap for his Stetson. He made sure his boots were clean, and he looked respectable. He pulled up in the church parking lot to meet Alison. She called him to say she'd have to meet him there as one of her clients needed her to come in before church to help her get ready since a family member was ill.

A dusting of snow speckled everything white. People ducked their heads against the wind as they headed inside the church. He should have gotten out of his truck and headed up those same stairs to wait for Alison, but this wasn't his church and he didn't feel right going in without her.

The folks at his parents' church knew too much about him and his epic failures, while his parents' praise landed on Jenny. No one at his current church held those against him, and the people here wouldn't know them.

He waited, watching for her car. She pulled in ten minutes later, and he got out to greet her.

Across the parking lot, he noticed the SUV that followed him into the ranch a few days earlier. He couldn't see, due to the collecting of snow on the windows, if someone sat inside it.

Alison's lovely blonde hair caught his attention as it spilled out around her knitted headband. "Hey, I've been anxious to see you!"

Josh offered his arm for her to take. "Missed me that much?" He winked.

"Maybe." She flirted back. "Did you find out anything about Gus?"

Helplessness rose up and caught him off guard. He looked forward to seeing her for days. He even put up with Jenny's sharp wit without making one remark back when she tried to rile him about coming here this morning. Before he knew it, she and Sarah would have him walking down the aisle and his mother knitting another blanket and booties. Not that the idea hadn't crossed his mind a time or two already.

He enjoyed going out on the trail ride, and much to his surprise, the older folks who went with him had a good time. He listened while they chatted, and it made him feel important leading the way. He followed the colored markers and noted in his mind places he'd like to go back and clean the trail or repaint the marks, as they faded. No one wanted to get lost, and he got the impression the trail ride had become an essential part of these people's social lives. Josh loved knowing it made all those folks happy, and it made Alison happy. She gave him an extra slice of apple crumb pie.

God had blessed her with the talent to look after others. Her faith humbled him, and he needed to have her in his life more often.

Which is why he figured on finding Alison's horse. If she believed Gus would come home as passionately as she believed in their Lord and Savior, then Josh believed, too. He also learned to pray because he couldn't do it alone.

Josh helped Alison up the stairs to the church. Someone had scattered salt to melt the ice accumulated over the night. Careful to step in places he was sure not to slip, he guided her inside. "Not yet, but it will."

He needed more time, and he wanted to sound confident for Alison.

He wouldn't give up, thinking he wouldn't be able to let it go if someone took his horse and knowing someone else would do the same for him to get it back. Josh planned to ask around at a few of the other livestock auctions as he made his monthly rounds of hauling and seeking new clients. He didn't want to share too much with her and risk adding to her burdens. She had too much on her plate. He could see that on his own.

Inside, he helped her remove her jacket and hung his hat on the peg.

Settled in a pew, Josh took Alison's hand and squeezed. He listened intently to the message. The pastor spoke of the road of temptations and trials. They sang one of Josh's favorites, "Turn Your Eyes Upon Jesus." Every once in a while, he felt as if someone was watching him — and not God's eyes, but another's boring in his back. He tried to dismiss it as visiting a new place.

After the service, Alison introduced him to an older woman, Mrs. Arnett, and several others whose faces blurred, and names wouldn't stick long after he followed her out of the church. They agreed to go in his truck, and he took her to lunch at the waffle house a few blocks from the church.

"I should order something and take it back to Gramps," Alison said as she looked at the menu.

"You look after him a lot, don't you?" Josh hadn't realized how much he respected Alison for the way she took care of her grandfather and her other clients. He could still see her standing there, pulling back a lock of her honey-blonde hair as she listened to Mrs. Arnett tell her about the latest antics of a dog, and one of the other ladies slipped her a jar of homemade apple butter and thanked her for doing her laundry the week before. All those people Alison helped, and it made him cherish the time she gave him.

"Someone has to." Alison laid down her menu. "It worries me he hasn't been out to see Mistress. Randy offered to take her over to Silver Wind's Animal Clinic to ensure she's comfortable and not suffering from that leg, but I know Gramps needs her there in the barn. He might not see her, but he will know she's gone."

"I agree. I've seen plenty of people come to the clinic who drop off pets and need closure. It would be better if he made a decision soon. I can talk to Michael about coming back out and checking on her. It isn't good for either of them to put off what needs doing." He took a sip of the coffee the waitress brought him with the menus.

"I'd appreciate it. I know Randy means well, but losing Mistress is like losing Gram again, you know?"

Josh took her hand in his. "I can't say I do. But I'm here for you, for you both. Whatever you need."

And he meant it.

When the waitress came and took their orders, Alison asked her to pack up one of the specials to go for Gramps. He couldn't take his eyes off her. Josh was in big trouble thinking he could help her and be friends with her again. No, he knew he wanted to kiss her, hold her in his arms, and have her lean on him when she needed strength.

"I can't tell you how much I appreciate that." Alison sipped at her coffee, a smile playing at her lips.

"What?" Josh leaned forward as if Alison knew a secret, and he wanted to be privy to it.

She waved her hand and kept hold of her coffee with the other. "Oh, nothing. It's just when I look at you. I don't see the old Josh I remember. You've changed."

"How's that?" he asked.

And she took another sip, seemed to think on how to answer him. He could see the twinkle in her eye as the waitress headed back their way with plates of waffles topped with whipped cream.

"Well, for one thing," she said. "You haven't put any straws up your nose or flirted with the waitress since we got here."

"Me?" he tried to seem offended. "I wouldn't." Then he grinned. "At least not with you sitting here." And he winked.

Alison shook her head. "There it is, the old Josh showing his colors."

"And what colors are those?" Because now, he did feel offended.

Alison shrugged. "The one who doesn't ever seem to have a care in the world or care about what others think of him. I used to like that about you."

"You shouldn't have." Josh leaned back, allowed the waitress to put their plates on the table and check if they needed anything else. "I'll be back with your to-go box in a bit."

"Thank you," Alison said as they waited for the older woman to step away to the next table.

Josh watched as Alison took her napkin and arranged it on her lap.

"Well, I did."

"I am not that same guy anymore, Ali. I take things seriously now." He waited while she took her silverware and started to arrange her waffles. "I like you, Ali."

She paused, mid-cut of her waffles. "I like you, too, Josh."

"I want to see you."

"You're seeing me right now."

"I don't mind coming out and lending a hand at the stables while your grandfather is healing. What I mean to ask is, when we can do this again? You and me?"

Alison's brows furrowed. "I don't know. My schedule is packed with the stables and the riding club, in addition to my clients. As you have seen. I don't have a regular nine-to-five job."

Relief eased him, as he feared she would come up with an excuse and turn him down. "Whatever you need me to do, Ali, say so and I'll make it work."

Chapter Seven

It must have been the sugar rush, or the cherry on top of the waffle she ordered on Sunday at lunch, that made her think she could date Josh Anderson. He'd been so sincere it stretched her heart to the point of pain to turn him down.

They agreed she would go with him out to Smithfield the Monday after next. The agency she worked for offered her another client and Alison had to turn them down. She knew they didn't have enough staff to call on all the people waiting for in-home care. Gramps wouldn't admit he liked having her around fussing over him between her other clients. Josh had started coming every morning and evening to help do the feeding. Several times she heard Randy grumbling about him getting things done in a different way than Randy's routine. Although, after this, nothing would ever go back to being the same again.

And then there was Mistress in her stall waiting for Gramps. Alison planned to try and encourage Gramps out of the house on one of the warmer days. As Wednesday rolled around, the weatherman's prediction brought them another six inches of snow, and two of the riding club members came down with the flu.

Alison made enough chicken broth and homemade fruit juice ice pops to have on stock for the season. She suspected Randy might be coming down with it since she noticed how sweaty and pale he'd become that morning and told him she'd take over for the evening feeding.

She looked forward to the evenings when Josh came to lend a hand. The man was always on the run, and she couldn't imagine he stayed in one place long or how he kept track of it all. Alison knew she had too many people to see on a daily basis, and without her phone calendar, she would end up at the wrong place and time. Either way, sometimes, knowing Josh would come in the evenings helped get her through the long days of grumpy clients and the gray winter days.

"Not one more cup of soup, you hear?" Gramps complained as she offered to get him something to eat before she headed to the barn.

"What else do you want?"

"Anything but soup," he grumbled.

Alison stood with her hands on her hips. "If you'd come out to the barn and see Mistress for a couple of minutes, I might be able to round up some of that lasagna we had a few days ago." Or a casserole, as there was plenty in the freezer from the good folks of the riding club and church.

"Don't try to bribe an old man."

"Gramps. You've been living in this chair since coming home from the hospital. I think you've seen every western there is and you saw them before, so you're not missing anything. Mistress has been standing out there in the barn, and you've always said never to keep a lady waiting. You've been keeping her on hold and me at the end of the line as we've needed you. At the very least, you can go see her."

Gramps scowled at her. "It's too cold."

"That's never stopped you before." Alison crossed her arms. "I'm not asking you to make a decision. I'm asking you to go see her. Josh has been looking after her by Dr. Kingsley's instructions as that leg of hers isn't going to heal right with her standing on it the way she is. And if it doesn't —"

Gramps held up his hand. "I don't need you to tell me. I know."

Alison let her arms drop to her side. She moved closer to Gramps's chair and knelt beside him. "I'm sorry. It's just not fair."

"What's not fair is you having to carry all the burden around here on your shoulders," Gramps said.

"I don't mind."

"I do." Gramps tossed the blanket off his legs. "You're right. Sharon would have given me a good dressing down on the first day home. She would have never let me leave that horse out there to suffer."

"Gram would have been too busy caring about you and getting you back on your feet."

Gramps grunted. "She would have taken action. Just like you." He pointed to Alison. "You're like your ma. A little honey bait to get a person motivated in the right direction."

"I don't want to rush you, Gramps, but I think you need to see Mistress as much as she's been missing you. She's not eating, and I think she's been looking for you."

"Of course she is, she's my mistress." His eyes watered a bit as he reached for Alison. "You get my cane, and I'll make it to my truck. You can drive me to the barn."

"I'll grab your coat."

Alison grabbed Gramps's coat and helped him into it. She had the truck keys off the hook by the door in seconds and gave Gramps all the patience he needed to see him safe and secure in the truck. She drove him to the barn, grinding a gear or two on the way.

Once there, Randy met them as he came around the corner of the stalls. Josh's truck sat parked on the side of the lane with his stock trailer hooked on the back. Randy marched up and got the door for Gramps, and the old man grunted, "What you think I am, an old woman?"

Alison took him by the arm. "He's upset I tipped him out of his warm nest on the recliner to come down here."

"I figured another day, and I was going to have to come up to the house and get you," Randy said.

"Nothing is stopping you." Gramps moved slow, and Alison kept hold in case he slipped. "Don't think I know what you're doing," he said to her.

Inside the barn, Gramps put a hand on the stall doors going down the row that led to Mistress. Alison went to go with him when Randy laid a hand on her shoulder. "You might want to go check in on that new boyfriend of yours."

"Boyfriend?" Alison giggled. She hadn't thought of Josh as her boyfriend, but it made her tingly and nervous at the same time.

Randy shrugged. "You know, the guy you got coming around here."

"Josh?" His name came out almost dreamlike, and she giggled.

Gramps grunted again. "Where's my mistress?"

At the sound of his voice, Mistress whinnied and stuck her nose through the bars of the stall door.

As if Josh heard, too, he came around the corner with a wheelbarrow filled from cleaning stalls.

"You're seeing him, aren't you?" Randy lowered his voice. His eyes narrowed on Josh.

An unsettling feeling crept into her bones. Alison stepped back from him. "While I appreciate your concern, my love life is my own."

"Got those last back row stalls done. You going to grab Hester and Tally?" Josh set down the wheelbarrow and whipped the sweat from his forehead.

"I'm getting there." Randy went over to Gramps, had a few words with him, and stalked off to get the horses. Josh winked at her, turned, and took the wheelbarrow to dump it behind the barn. "I'll be back in a moment."

She nodded, watching as Gramps fumbled with the stall lock. Quickly, she moved to help, then caught herself. Gramps got it, and they slid the door to the side together. Gramps's face turned a little peaked, and his eyes got watery again. He grabbed hold of Mistress's halter, keeping the mare from stumbling forward. "Whoa there, Mistress. I missed you, too."

Alison stepped in front of the horse to protect Gramps. The last thing they both needed was for Gramps to take a trip back to the hospital. Gramps ran his hand down the horse's blaze. Mistress bobbed her head, and Gramps patted the horse's neck. "I'm here now. It's going to be okay."

Then Gramps gave her a nudge. "You go on now. Mistress and I would like a minute or two. Go find that *boyfriend* of yours."

Alison opened her mouth to protest, then spotted Josh coming back in the barn. She kissed Gramps on the cheek. "If you need me, I won't be far."

"Everything okay?" Josh parked the wheelbarrow back in the storage stall. She stepped in with him, lowering her voice. "I hope so. Gramps finally decided to come out, but I don't think he was up to it yet, and I pushed him a little to get him out here."

Josh pulled her in his arms for a hug. "I'm glad you did."

"Why's that?"

"Michael's been concerned about the bones trying to knit as they are or the break getting worse. He never figured your Gramps would take this long."

"I know." Guilt plagued her for not forcing Gramps out here sooner. A few times she'd thought to make the call herself, but couldn't take the decision away from Gramps. She prayed these past few days he would do what was right, and in her heart, she believed he would. She believed in her heart she'd one day see her beloved horse, Gus, again, too.

Her emotions had a way of getting the best of her, and she reached up to brush away a stray tear that had slipped over her cheek.

"Hey, now." Josh hugged her tighter. "No need to go crying. You don't know what is going to happen."

"It's just how I get. At least Gramps gets to say goodbye when the time comes."

Alison's phone chimed, and she pulled it from her jacket pocket. She almost dropped it when she saw Jason's face appear on the incoming message screen. Quickly, she shoved it back in her pocket. A second later, the phone rang, and she chose to ignore it.

"Aren't you going to answer?"

"It's not important." Her phone vibrated, signaling the call went to her voice messages. Later, when Josh wasn't around, she'd delete it. No matter what Jason had to say, she didn't want to speak with him anymore. He'd try to convince her to come back and give it another chance, but things would end up the same way they always did with him.

Josh stepped away from her the moment the barn doors slid open, letting a gust of cold sweep into the barn. She stuck her hand in her pocket over the phone. Maybe she should check it. After all, it could be a client, but Alison shook her head and followed Josh as he walked out to the open doors to meet Randy. He took Tally, Mr. Gavin's chestnut horse, by the lead. Randy offered her the other one, so she took Hester, a pretty black pony of Mrs. Crofts.

While they put away the horses, she heard Randy speaking with Gramps. The stall door slid shut, and Alison's heart squeezed with the bang of the metal latch sliding in the lock.

"Young man. I'll have a word," Gramps called.

Josh glanced at her, and Alison shook her head. She followed behind him, curiosity getting the best of her. In her pocket, her phone rang, but she ignored it.

"Yes, sir?" Josh approached Gramps. She had to admire a man with that kind of respect in his voice.

Randy stood beside Gramps, looking deflated. Alison sympathized with the older man. She knew that look and understood whatever Randy had tried to talk Gramps out of doing hadn't worked.

"I see you got that trailer hooked up to your truck," Gramps said.

"I do. I have a team of horses I need to transport after I leave here."

"So, you don't have any more time for anything else today?" Gramps asked.

Josh pulled off his work gloves. "Depends on what you had in mind."

"What's in your head, Gramps?" Alison asked, her phone buzzing as another message went to voice. She would deal with Jason later, or preferably not at all. Why couldn't he accept they were over? She threw a silent prayer to God for Jason to stop calling her, and for whatever Gramps had in his head to do was the right thing because something deep in her heart became troubled.

"I am trying to tell him it's not a good idea," Randy said.

"Stop trying to be a good friend. I know what's best for my mistress." Gramps shuffled closer to Josh as if he sized him up for the job, and Alison tried not to giggle.

"You want me to take Mistress to the clinic?" Josh asked.

Gramps coughed. "You tell that new modern vet to handle her with care, no more suffering, you hear?"

Alison caught the sob in her throat. Josh reached for her, and she clung to Gramps.

"Are you sure?" she whispered.

"Not you, too." Gramps patted Alison's arm and looked at Josh. "You load her up. If you need help, Randy has agreed to help you get her on the trailer, but later, when you've got time. I figure it will be easier on my mistress if I'm not here, we've said our goodbyes for now." Gramps glanced over at Mistress, his chin quivering. Alison's heart went out to him, trying to hold strong. Her phone went off again, and she ignored it.

"She'll be in good hands." Josh moved to allow Gramps to shuffle past. Alison helped him as he moved along. Gramps shrugged her from his arm. "Alison, girl. I know you mean well, but a man can walk out of his own barn without you hanging on him."

Shocked by the gruffness in his voice, Alison released him.

"And answer your phone, it's buzzing is enough to drive a man crazy." She reached in her pocket for the buzzing phone.

"I'll see him up to the house." Randy walked past her. Alison stood staring after the two old men.

Josh leaned into her shoulder. "He's right, you know."

"What?" She clutched the phone, her grip tightening around it. She glared at him, furious at the way she allowed Gramps to make her feel, and more upset to have Josh rubbing it in.

"The phone." Josh pointed. "It keeps ringing. Maybe you should see who is trying to get a hold of you. Might be important."

"I know who it is." Her emotions ran on high. She held up the phone and gasped. It was her manager calling from the home health agency where she worked. She'd missed three calls from them. Panic started to rise as she hit the call back button. Josh stood, watching, and waiting patiently as she turned away.

"Hello."

"Rochelle? It's Alison."

"Girl, where have you been? I've been trying to get a hold of you."

Alison wrapped her arm around her waist. "Sorry. What's up?"

"Mrs. Crawford's daughter called. She tried to call you, but some guy answered and freaked her out. It wasn't you."

"She must have used my old number that Jason has now. It probably got forwarded to his phone." Alison put her hand on her face. She never thought to make sure everyone had updated phone numbers when she gave Jason back the phone and become more independent from him.

"What's wrong?"

"She's not calling for a social chat." Rochelle's voice went serious. "Mrs. Crawford is dead. She was lying on the floor in the bedroom when the daughter found her a few hours ago."

"No." Alison spun around, stared at Josh, all the blood left her head, and she could barely think. "I just saw her this morning."

"Her daughter is questioning her care. She wanted to know why her mother was still in bed when she should have been in her chair."

Alison shook her head, realized Rochelle couldn't see her, and said, "She was in her chair when I left her this morning. She had a new ball of tan yarn and was knitting a prayer shawl for the ladies' ministry at church. She had a cough, but most of our clients do with the cold and flu going around. She was fine when I left her."

"I'm sorry, Alison. I'll need your paperwork in the office by morning. If you can send it over to me the sooner, the better. It's never easy when we lose loved ones. I'm sure once the daughter is able to process the loss, all things will be okay. I know you're quite close with Mrs. Crawford."

"She's been my client for years." Alison's brain couldn't count how many at this moment.

Tears built up behind her eyes. Josh frowned, holding his arms out to her.

She barely heard the rest of the conversation before Rochelle hung up.

"I lost a client. I just saw her this morning and now — she's — gone."

"As in, she passed?"

Alison nodded as Josh pulled her into his embrace. It seemed he was doing that a lot lately. Always there, always holding her, and she couldn't think of anyone else she would rather have hold her. She allowed herself to cry. Mrs. Crawford was like another grandmother to her. How could she have not seen it coming?

Josh laid his cheek close to hers and let her cry. Somewhere in the grief crashing over her, she could hear his soft words of prayer for the Crawford family, and it gave her a comforting sense of peace.

Chapter Eight

On Monday evening, Josh stood outside on the porch as he listened to Dwight Vandergraft tell Alison to be on her way. The older man's gruff voice floated out past the living room windows. Josh tapped his feet a little to keep the cold from getting inside his boots.

Alison offered for him to come in, but he would just as soon wait outside for her. Not that Dwight had said a thing to him, and ever since Josh had loaded up Mistress, he could see the sadness in the older man's eyes. It was the same kind of sorrow he saw flicker in Alison's gaze when they worked together in the barn when he came over to lend a hand.

He didn't want to remind the older gentleman of saying goodbye to his horse any more than he wanted to see Alison grieving the one that had been stolen. He talked to Sarah about digging deeper into her connections with the authorities and humane society to try and find Alison's horse. He thought about offering a reward, but Dwight had done that, and nothing had come about.

Cade warned him to stay out of trouble, not to go looking for answering in desperation, and of course, Jenny reminded him that God knew where Alison's horse was, and there was a purpose for all this. Josh prayed God knew what He was doing, but Josh sure didn't.

A few moments later, Alison stepped out on the porch. She wore a wool-lined cable sweater and faded pair of jeans. He liked it when she wore her hair down around her shoulders, and she'd swiped some pink gloss on her lips. Watermelon, he figured by the scent when he leaned close to her.

"All ready?"

"Ready."

A man could get used to a smile like that, one that made the sun seem dim in comparison. He took her hand as they walked to the truck.

"Are you sure you want to come with me tonight?"

He had doubts about the last couple of days. He almost skipped out on going tonight by telling Alison he had other work he needed to finish. It wouldn't have been a lie. Jenny had gotten on his case about turning down going out on farm calls with Michael in the mornings to get his work finished at the stables and the clinic to help Alison and her grandfather. Randy seemed to accept his help, although the man scowled more than he smiled and grunted and barked orders more like a foreman than a volunteer stable manager. Josh understood Randy wanting to step in and make sure all was well with the stables, with Dwight healing in the house and Alison going back and forth between her clients and the barn. Josh wished he could do more, and quite frankly, he had to admit he looked forward to leading the trail ride again this week.

Ole Texas seemed the perfect fit for Maddy Pierce. The older woman came twice a week and on trail days to visit and ride Texas. Instead of the riding club adopting the seasoned gelding, Maddy had inquired about adopting the horse herself.

The ride to the livestock auction in Smithfield stretched in silence until Josh fiddled with the heat settings in the cab, and Alison assured him she was plenty warm. He never knew if it would throw hot air or cold and grabbed a blanket in case it turned chilly on the ride. He meant to get it fixed, but every last dollar he earned, he used to pay Cade back from getting him out of his gambling debts last year.

"I'm working tonight, I won't be able to sit with you, but if you pick a place down in front, I can hang close."

"I know, and I don't mind. I told you before I was willing to try to make this work. I am happy to spend time with you, Josh."

He reached over and entwined her fingers with his. "I appreciate that, Ali. I have to admit. I've screwed up a lot of things in my life, and this," he gave her hand an extra squeeze, "is one of those things I want to get right."

"You know I've always wondered why you never spoke to me again after that summer. I'd be lying if I didn't say it hurt. It crushed me. And now, here you are back in my life, and I am still trying to figure this out. Us."

Josh dared a glance at her as he came near the turn into the parking lot near the livestock auction barn. "I screwed up. Something happened, and it wasn't your fault. It was mine. I didn't know how to explain, and I knew I'd hurt you more, and it was complicated."

Alison turned, facing him. She placed her other hand over his, and he had to use it to shift gears as he slowed and found a place to park. She waited as he pulled his truck and trailer in line with a few others parked along the auction barn.

"I told myself a dozen times it's in the past, but I need to know. We were young, I get that, but what made you not talk to me all these years?"

Her voice was soft, and those big beautiful eyes of hers could gut a man. He made sure to put on the parking brake and said, "It was Sarah."

"Sarah?" She didn't pull away from him like he figured she would. "You and Sarah? She dropped out of school, didn't she? And her son belongs to Dr. Kingsley. Well, both their sons."

Alison clamped her lips together with a pained expression on her face.

"You're right. Sarah dropped out of school when she got pregnant with her and Michael's first son. I felt responsible. Sarah is my sister's best friend, and I was sent to look after my sister that summer while we worked at Kingsleys' estate."

"It's so like you." She shook her head. "You don't have to tell me any more. For the longest time, I figured you found someone else, and Jenny kinda made me feel you had, so I figured it was better not to try and find out from you myself if you had someone else."

"Jenny? You talked to my sister?" Josh was more annoyed with Jenny than ever. He should have known she would have had a say in part of his life, no matter what.

"Before I agreed to go steady with Jason. Seems silly now when you think of 'going steady' with someone. I wanted to make sure I hadn't misread your silent treatment and wanted to be sure there wasn't any chance of you getting mad at me."

Josh laughed. He grabbed Alison by the face and planted a big kiss on her lips. "Mad at you? Ali, you should have been furious with me! I'm the one who didn't deserve you then, and I'm trying to be the man you deserve now."

Alison brushed her lips against his. "I know who you are, Josh Anderson. It might have been years since we have seen each other or spoke, but nothing much changes."

"I have. And I'll prove it to you." Josh slid away, got out of the truck, and came around to open the door for her.

"I always knew you were a gentleman." Alison got out of the truck. "When you want to be."

"Those are flirting words, woman." He shut the door and took her hand in his. "You keep talking to me like that, and we'll miss the auction."

Alison giggled and gave him a playful punch in the arm. Unable to resist, Josh leaned over and kissed her again. This time slowly, he savored the feel of her lips and the slight taste of her watermelon lip gloss. She tilted her head, invited him to kiss her longer, stepped closer into his arms, and made Josh the happiest he could ever remember.

Inside, he found a spot for Alison down front where he could slip to the side and stand close to her when the livestock moved around the sale ring. Through the night, she grabbed him a coffee, and when the last of the yearlings went through, Alison got up and hadn't returned in some time.

Josh waited a bit, wondering if she went for coffee or needed the ladies' room. When three more animals went through, and she didn't return, Josh handed his training stick to Clem Johnson. "I'll be back."

The other man shouted from the back, and young Ben, the auctioneer's son, took Josh's place while he headed to find Alison.

As he weaved through the pens of horses and came to the stairs, he spotted her walking across the planked walkway above the pens. She stood at the end, leaning toward where the back doors were open, and some men brought in some horses for later in the sale.

As he moved closer, he tipped back his hat and said a prayer under his breath. Alison tensed and jumped a little at the sound of his voice. "I got worried."

"I needed to stretch my legs." Alison pointed out toward where the men were struggling to get a white horse off the trailer. "They've been trying to get him off for a bit now."

Josh followed his gaze. The horse was white and caked with mud. It had splattered brown spots, and he could tell by Alison's tense stature she might be holding her breath.

Josh put his arm around her. He knew he needed to get back to the ring soon, but Ben could stand in for him for a few more minutes. He recognized the truck and knew the man who owned it.

His gut turned sour, and he tried to turn Alison away. "There's a mare and her foal in the front getting ready to come out on the block soon. It's a pretty little filly. I thought you might want to see."

But Alison wouldn't be swayed. "Maybe we should go down there and help them."

"Only staff is allowed down in the pens. Besides, Jimmy is down there. It's best to let the owner handle unloading them."

"Did you see the horse?" Alison asked.

Josh pressed his hand to her back. "It's a dirty white horse."

"It could be Gus."

Josh took a long hard look at the horse. It was dark outside, and the fluorescent bulb hanging from the ceiling of the barn didn't light the place up good enough to see in the shadows.

This had been one of the reasons he had doubts about bringing her. Selfish as it was, he wanted to be close to her.

"I'll go down and take a look when they get it settled. There comes Jimmy now." Josh pointed to a man in a stained plaid shirt and bald spot on his head.

"You go on, and I'll stay and watch. I'll go back in when I see it come out."

Josh shook his head. "It's not Gus."

At the dock, the trailer shook, and the horse kicked the side of the aluminum wall. Josh saw wild ones like this before. A man went around the trailer and came back with a rope. More squealing and kicking came from the shadows inside the trailer. It would get rough. For Alison's sake, he hoped the horse would bolt and run off the trailer without much more fuss.

"Hey, Jim! Whatcha got down there?" Josh moved from Alison and leaned over to shout down at the man.

"One mad mare!" Jimmy yelled. "You done in the ring?"

"On my way back now!"

"Lucky you!" Jimmy turned away and focused on the horse.

Josh took Alison by the hand. A few yells and an agitated whine came from below. The horse bolted out of the trailer. A tall, skinny mare whirled around, teeth and hooves flying as the men hurried to shut a gate so it couldn't run back in, while another man ran ahead to open gates and direct the horse into a pen.

Alison walked down the floating boardwalk above the pens and watched as the horse twisted, turned, and kicked inside the pen. "What's wrong with the horse?"

"Afraid." Josh wrapped his arms around her waist and pulled her back against him. Ben needed some experience in the ring, and if Clem said anything he'd tell him so. Alison needed him more this moment.

"She'll calm down soon. Being in a strange place and unfamiliar scents spook a horse. That mare probably hasn't had anyone paying attention to her in a while. They get a little wild when you let them loose and don't spend time with them every day."

Alison hugged herself. "When she first stuck her head out, I got this jolt of hope, you know. She could have been him. I thought I saw my Gus."

If only it were that easy. Josh kissed her hair. He couldn't bring himself to tell her the chances of finding her leopard Appaloosa were slim, and in a place like this, the horse could have passed hands and gone states away in a matter of days for all kinds of purposes.

She'd lost too much already. He could hear it in the weariness of her voice. "Come on. I've got to get back."

"I'd like to stay here for a bit. You go on."

He took it. She wanted some time to sort away the emotions. He understood as he often needed the same thing.

When the auctioneer announced they were moving to the workhorses, reluctantly, Josh released her. "We can leave now, and I can take you home."

"You're working."

"I don't care. I told you in the truck on the way here. I'm not going to screw this up again. I don't suppose I'll get more than a second chance every day, and I aim to keep it right between us."

Alison snuggled into his arms, laid her cheek against his shoulder. "I'm glad God brought you back into my life. It's the only thing that's felt right in a long time."

Chapter Nine

By three o'clock on Wednesday afternoon, Alison had heard more goodbyes than one person ought to endure. Mrs. Crawford's memorial service included the reading of the woman's will. To her daughter's great displeasure, the cat got the house, and her daughter would have to care for the cat in order to gain the holdings. She could almost hear Mrs. Crawford clucking from heaven and found it sweet and amusing at the same time to have inherited Mrs. Crawford's house plants. Mrs. Crawford hadn't heard her well when Alison tried telling her last year that house plants were not her friend.

But Mrs. Crawford was, and Alison's heart hurt with the loss of seeing her every day.

Do not let your hearts be troubled, came to mind as she gathered the plants and put them in her car, and while she tried to recall the other part of the scripture. Her mind on the scripture and those in the Silver Stirrups Riding Club out on the trail, she didn't notice Jason coming across the parking lot with his umbrella overhead. It hid part of his face until he picked up the remaining house plant she'd sat on the curb and held it out to her.

Of all the days for Mrs. Crawford's daughter to choose for a memorial, a steady drizzle of rain had started that morning and refused to let up.

Guilt would keep her from donating the plants to someone who could care for them better, just as guilt would keep her from getting in her car and slamming the door without speaking to him. Her parents raised her better than this, and Gramps would give her a disapproving frown. She knew Jason had called him to check on Gramps. She knew, too, Gramps believed in forgiveness and second chances.

"How are you?"

They'd had their second chance, and by the concern oozing from his voice, he came with an intention.

"Who told you I was here?" Alison placed the plants in the back floor space of her vehicle. She took the one Jason held out for her.

"My mom works with Gail."

Their circles would always cross. She had to accept that. She suspected talking to him wasn't the end of the world. They had, after all, been together for many years.

And she missed him, the good times they had. The man he wanted to show her, and the one she believed he was. It brought the sting back, not in an angry or painful sort of way. More like a splinter, and she sighed. He genuinely seemed like he cared.

"You missed the service and the reading of the will."

"I couldn't get off work. I took a late lunch. I wanted to see how you were doing." Jason tried to move closer, and Alison stepped back. He held out his umbrella to keep her from getting wetter if that was even possible.

"You know how attached I get to my grandmas. As you can see, Mrs. Crawford has faith in my green thumb."

Jason chuckled at that. "Did you tell her about the time you house-sat that philodendron for your client when she went to Florida for a month?"

"You remember?" Alison asked, astonished he would mention it, let alone remember it.

Jason grinned. "Poor thing, you drowned it with watering it every day."

"I did." Alison had no idea how Mrs. Crawford's plants were going to survive. Jason had always been the one to do better with plants. "Maybe you should take one of these. I'd hate to be the one to kill them all, as unintentional as it would be."

"I'd take them all, Alison," Jason's voice turned husky, "if it would mean you coming by to check on them once in a while."

"Maybe if I hang them near the windows in the barn. One of the club members might have a talent for plants and enjoy tending them."

His face hardened, and his eyes narrowed. She hadn't said what he wanted to hear. Alison reached for her car door, bracing herself for his reaction.

Cool and calmly, Jason said, "I miss you."

What could she say to that? Silently she sent up a prayer for escape and Jason. She chewed on her lip, trying to find the right thing to say.

"I miss you." He repeated it. "Give me another chance. I'll make it right this time. I'll get Gus back."

A cold tingle slid down Alison's spine. Josh had told her the same thing. He wanted to do right by her. She could tell Josh wanted to make up for the past. More than that, he felt he needed to prove himself worthy of her love.

And she did love — Josh. Oh Lord, it was there all along. Josh had come back into her life for a few short weeks, and her heart recognized him before she had. What would he think when she told him he was God's perfect gift to her?

"Alison?" Jason's voice snapped her out of her realization. He held the umbrella over her, standing nose to nose with her. His eyes filled with expectation, and behind them the flicker of his true self.

"I've told you. Please accept that we've run out of chances. Move on, Jason. I have."

"You'd be willing to give up on us even if it means getting Gus back?" He leaned in closer to her.

Alison pushed him back. "What about Gus?"

"We'll speak of it more this evening. I'll pick you up at seven. Missy, Sean, and Chelsea are meeting at Thornton's."

"No," Alison said firmly. "You go."

"And sit with a bunch of other people while you go out with your boyfriend?" Jason clenched his jaw.

"I know you've been talking to Gramps. I won't deny I'm dating Josh. He's helping me find Gus."

"I'm the only one who can help you find Gus. Do you understand? Dump the loser and come with me tonight. I'll forgive you, and we'll get Gus back. Together."

"You know something about Gus?"

Alison watched with horror as Jason's lips formed a smirk. His eyes flashed like they always did when he was about to get his way. And her insides went to ice as he said, "Be ready by quarter after six since I have to drive the whole way out to that farm place to pick you up."

Long after Jason strolled away, Alison sat in her car and watched the drops of rain roll down the windshield. Twice she picked up her phone and went to press the button to call Josh, and twice she put the phone down.

She couldn't remember turning on the car or driving back to Windy Knoll, or parking by the house. Relieved not to see Josh's truck, she went into the house. About halfway to the porch, she remembered the house plants. One by one, she set them on the porch. At least they'd get a little rain while her mind fussed with a much bigger dilemma.

Deep down, she suspected Jason had something to do with Gus's disappearance. Ashamed of thinking the worst of the man she loved for so many years, she pushed it aside. Jason had done many things, and it shouldn't surprise her that he'd go this low.

But it did.

Centered in the pit of her stomach, a slow burn had started somewhere between town and turning down the lane. On top of it, the weight of her own naivete sent a ripple of humiliation.

"So much for giving others the benefit of the doubt," Alison muttered, going into the house. As she hung her coat and went into the living room, she froze. The house was quiet. She realized the television wasn't on. And Gramps wasn't in his chair.

"Gramps?" She went into the kitchen with relief washing over her. Gramps looked up from smearing jam on a piece of bread. "That home care woman called here looking for you. Wants you to be out at the Fredrickson place at four. She texted you."

Alison looked at her phone. She had ignored it on the ride and gave herself a mental shake. It wasn't like her not paying attention to her phone and missing calls or texts when her job relied on her to be alert. "I'm guessing Nadine came down with the flu. She usually takes care of

Mr. Frederickson. It's almost four now. I'd better head to the barn and check in with Randy."

Gramps waved his hand. "You can leave to make one man supper, but you can't help out your Gramps."

He had humor in his rough voice, but it made Alison agitated. "Mr. Frederickson can't walk, Gramps. Shame on you. Besides, if you can get up and move around to make a sandwich you can heat the portion of leftover soup in the fridge to go with it."

Gramps frowned. "You don't want me to wait for you?"

"Not tonight. I fear I've been blackmailed into going out tonight with Jason."

The butter knife in Gramps's hand clattered on the counter. "Jason? What happened to Josh?"

"Nothing." Alison put down her purse and sat at the counter for a minute. "Yet."

"Spill it. You know you need to." Gramps took his sandwich and shuffled toward the living room, "But you'll need to do it in here. I might be able to stand, but I still need to rest in my chair."

Alison followed him to his chair, helped him settle, but didn't sit. It seemed she never had a moment to sit down anymore.

"I saw Jason today."

"I figured as much." Gramps rested his head back. "He's been trying awful hard to get on my good side. He asked if he could come over on Sunday for dinner like old times and I told him I didn't think it would be a good idea. Especially since your *boyfriend* would be at the table, too."

Randy had been coming up to the house more and more these days to visit with Gramps while she worked.

"Gramps," Alison started to say when Gramps held up his sandwich.

"Alison. You like Josh."

"I think I love him, Gramps."

"Then why are you letting Jason get in the way?" Gramps bit into the sandwich.

"I think he knows where Gus is."

Gramps chewed thoughtfully, then said, "He told you that."

Alison nodded. "He said he was the only one who could help me find Gus. And he knew I had a boyfriend."

Gramps looked sheepish. "Fellow doesn't know how to take a hint, does he?"

"I have to find out if he knows where Gus is."

"What about Josh?"

"He'll understand." Alison kissed Gramps on the cheek and headed to the door.

"I'm sure he will," Gramps said and clicked on the television. Gramps didn't sound too convinced.

Down at the barn, Alison made quick notes of what needed to be done. On the chalkboard outside the feed room, she left instructions. It didn't take long before she walked past Mistress's empty stall and couldn't help the avalanche of grief rolling down through her chest.

Everything had its time. God brought people into her life when she needed them and then left when a new season came along. Her grandmother would have said that, and if she dialed and called her mother, she'd confirm it. Her parents didn't need her calling and weeping because of a bad day.

She talked to her mother once a week on Alison's drive out to the McGarvey place each Thursday after seeing Mrs. Crawford. Only that routine would change as Mrs. Crawford no longer needed Alison. She'd gone to be with the Lord, and like many other clients she had over the years, Alison would find peace in it. She was blessed by the time she had with the folks she cared for in her job.

They were more than assignments, they were people she came to think of as extra sets of grandparents, and she loved them as such.

Lord knew how much it hurt to lose them. She moved away from the stall and headed back to the doors to try and shake away her bout of melancholy.

Maddy Pierce's voice rang out as the woman walked toward the barn and waved. Her cheeks were flushed pink, but she had a bright smile. "Hello there, Alison. We missed you on the ride!"

"Did you go?" Alison went to greet her.

Maddy was a medium-built woman with salt and pepper in her hair and was a little timid.

"Oh, I did!" Maddy looked the happiest Alison had seen the older woman in ages. "Did Josh tell you I'm going to adopt Texas?"

"I believe it was mentioned." Alison hugged the woman as she held out her arms. Everyone needed a hug now and then, and it seemed Maddy had come at the right time. The woman's joy seemed to fill Alison, too, and chase away her darker mood from moments ago.

"I'll be keeping him here, of course."

"Of course."

"I went up and saw Dwight after the ride today. He's looking good. Although I have to admit, I told him not to hurry on getting back to the trail." Maddy talked as they went back inside the barn to shelter from the cool breeze coming across the fields. "I feel bad about his mistress. It'll be hard coming back out here, but that new trail master you hired is an inspiration, if you know what I mean."

Maddy winked.

And Alison giggled.

"Josh is volunteering. We appreciate all the time he's been giving to help the Silver Stirrups and here at the barn."

"Well, we appreciate him." Maddy grinned. "Do you know he holds that steppy mare of his back on the trail and instead of leading, sometimes falls back and lets each of us take a turn at going through certain parts first."

"I didn't."

"He's got a way with him, that young man, got a good head and respect. You'd be wise to keep him around," Maddy said.

"I think we can arrange that." Alison had no intention of letting Josh walk away from her again. Maddy pulled a carrot out of her pocket. "I promised Texas a treat and wanted to stop by to give it to him."

"You'll spoil his supper," Randy's voice boomed from the doorway.

"Oh, pish-posh," Maddy waved her hand, and Alison realized the time had grown late. She would have to hurry along, so she was back in time for Jason to pick her up. Or maybe she could call him and meet him there since she had to go on an unexpected visit.

"I hate to run, but I have a client to see last minute. Randy, can you handle things here? I have somewhere else I have to go after, and I might not return until late."

Randy grunted. "Go on. I've managed before by myself."

"Josh will be coming. Will you tell him ..." Alison paused, tried to think how to explain it to him. "I'll see him tomorrow."

"Is there anything I can do?" Maddy asked.

Randy took a good long look at the other woman and scowled. "You know how to measure feed?"

"I know how to measure to bake, is it the same?"

"Mostly," Alison said. "Thank you so much."

"You go on. We'll figure this out," Maddy said. "Good luck with that home visit."

"Don't be staying out too late tonight with your friends," Randy said.

They weren't her friends. They were Jason's. She opened her mouth to tell him, then thought better of it. The less others knew of this situation, the better. She hurried to go on her way.

She would have a much better time if she were seeing Josh, but Alison cringed, wanting to get this over with and done.

For Gus, she thought, praying she was doing the right thing.

Chapter Ten

It was almost nine when Josh pulled into Thornton's to grab some takeout and see if Alison wanted to go stargazing with him.

He texted her several times throughout the day to say he missed her, was thinking of her. Especially since he figured today had to be one of the hardest days she would endure with Mrs. Crawford's memorial. He wanted to go, but she made him promise to see the members of the Silver Stirrups Riding Club had a good and safe ride. Despite the constant drizzle, those folks were saddled and ready to go. They took one of the shorter and easier trails as his mind seemed focused on Alison much of the time.

The rescue pulled him away for most of the afternoon and evening, and he called the stables to let Randy know he wouldn't make it this evening.

Feeling guilty and yearning to hold Alison in his arms, he decided to surprise her. Wednesday night happy hour at Thorton's also consisted of cheap wings and fries, so he called and ordered ahead to go.

Laughter and music floated through the bar when Josh strolled through to pick up his order. He went in on the food side, grinned as Sheila held up her hand for him to wait a minute while she finished taking an order on the phone. Josh moved over a bit and took a look in the bar to see what band played. The whole bar scene thing might have been a place he went a few years ago, but not anymore. He grabbed his food and got ready to go when he heard a familiar giggle.

She was standing in a group of people, swaying her hips to the music, and Josh had to look twice to recognize Alison. A man slid his hand around her waist, and Josh waited for Alison to step away. When she didn't, he clutched the bag of food a bit tighter, especially when Jason's face turned, and Josh saw her with him.

He turned on his heel and marched out of there and tossed the food on the seat of his truck, no longer hungry.

Josh spent the night staring at his phone. He texted her, then deleted it and couldn't decide what to say. Finally, by midnight, he gave up and got some shut-eye.

In the morning, he went over to the clinic, where Jenny yawned and didn't seem to look a mite better than he did. "Coffee?"

She groaned, placing her hands on her hips to tilt back and stretch. "Please."

"I won't tell you, you look awful," he said.

Jenny ignored him. She'd let her hair grow longer and had it pulled back in a small ponytail. He grabbed them both a cup of coffee and brought it the way she liked it, extra sugar and no milk. Josh preferred his black this morning.

"Looks like your many lives are catching up to you." She took the coffee and settled into her office chair. Josh sat on the edge of her desk, and for once, she didn't seem to mind.

"Can we skip the chit chat and get to the part where you tell me what to do today?" Josh winced when he saw the hurt look on Jenny's face. Usually, she'd have some snarky reply. What was wrong with people today?

He took another deep gulp of his coffee and apologized. "Rough night."

Jenny looked like she was about to cry.

"Hey, I said I'm sorry."

Jenny shook her head. "It's the baby. I can't sleep at night. I toss and turn, and then when I get comfortable, he kicks my bladder!"

"Cade or the baby?" Josh wanted to make sure he understood.

"The baby." She gave him the stink eye. "What's your excuse?"

"Been busy."

"You need to slow down." Jenny reached over and took a paper from the printer and handed it to him. "Cade went with Michael this morning, so you'll need to fill in for him over at the rescue."

Josh took the paper and scanned the instructions. Ever since Jenny started managing the clinic, they'd gone from verbal instructions to writing things on a whiteboard, to print outs. Not that he needed to listen to her. Sarah ran the rescue. He took his time sipping his coffee and reading the list: stalls to clean, horses to exercise, a gate to fix at the rescue, and more stalls and feeding at the clinic.

"You should be able to get that done and have time to make it over to Windy Knoll by feeding time."

"I have cows to haul to the buyers' station this afternoon. I don't know if I'll get this all done."

Jenny crossed her arms. "Then you'll have to cancel."

"I can't cancel. The buyers' station is only open on Thursdays."

"Then you'll have to tell Alison you can't be going over to Windy Knoll every day. I understand her grandfather is recovering and needs a hand, but you're also needed here. You've got to stop doing so many things. Have you ever thought about picking one thing and sticking to it?"

"You sound like Dad." Josh finished his coffee and moved away from the desk. "I'll start on the clinic stalls this morning and run the cattle to the buyer's station at lunch. When I get back, I'll head over to the rescue, and if it takes me until midnight, I'll get my job done."

"What about Windy Knoll?" Jenny asked.

"She's hanging back with her ex. She can have him help her out." He tried to keep the bitterness from seeping in.

Jenny's eyes widened. "Did she tell you that?"

"I saw them last night together at Thornton's. He had his arm around her."

Jenny tilted her head and looked him hard in the eye. "Were they on a date or with a bunch of people?"

"Makes no difference. He had his arm around her, and she was in the bar section." Alison didn't do bars. She didn't drink. He knew that from when they were younger, but all night long, he couldn't help thinking he might not have been the only one to change in the time they'd been apart. He couldn't rub away the sting it caused.

"If you had come to church with us last Sunday, you would have heard the visiting pastor say that one shouldn't judge others, or you, too, shall be judged in the same measure."

"I've been at Alison's church these past few Sundays. No one knows me well, and they accept me. I like it there." He wouldn't mention sometimes he felt like they were being watched. He imagined it was God looking down on them, ready to strike His wrath when Josh screwed up, but then he reminded himself God loved His children, even when they did wrong.

What had he done to make Alison go out with her ex again? She texted this morning asking to have lunch. Even if he could find the time for it in his schedule today, he turned her down.

"Mom and Dad have been asking about you. Maybe once a month you could come to church again with us if you're going to continue going there. Mom's been trying new recipes, and even Cade complimented her on her roast chicken last time. Maybe this Sunday?"

"Yeah. I'll come this Sunday." He wondered how long into dinner before his dad asked him when he would get a real job. He'd looked forward to bringing Alison to Sunday dinner. She'd like his mom, or at least his mom would get along with her.

Not that it mattered at the moment.

"Don't forget, we're having supper at the farmhouse tonight."

That was Michael and Sarah's place.

Josh left his sister as a man and woman came in with four small fluffy dogs in their arms. It must be Doc Miller's day to see patients in the clinic.

It was getting warm in the barn. The sun had been out all day, and the snow had about all melted before the sun decided to disappear. Josh patted Destiny on the neck and put her back in her stall. He took her over to Windy Knoll these past Wednesdays to ride the trail with the Silver Stirrups, and he managed to get Texas adopted by Maddy Pierce.

Sarah wanted to keep Destiny back in the stables where Cade could work with her more if Windy Knoll wasn't interested in keeping the mare. Sarah tried hard to find every horse a home, and Josh admired that. But, giving up Destiny to someone else had started to bother him.

He hated to admit that he'd grown attached to the leggy thoroughbred.

91

"Looks like we're the last to get our supper tonight." He shut the stall door while Destiny went straight for her feed box. He brushed the sawdust from his coat. As he came around the corner of the stalls, Alison stood by the door.

His throat tightened, holding back any words. Not that he had any to say to her. It took most of the day for him to think about it. Too little sleep had his mind racing, and he figured after a good night's sleep, he could make more sense of what was going on.

His sister had been right. He couldn't keep going at this pace. He turned down an extra hauling job today to take care of what he had on his plate, and even then, he hadn't made it over to help at Windy Knoll.

Alison had tried to call him, texted him a few times, and here she stood.

"Sarah said to tell you to come in when you're done. The chili is hot, and you can grab a bowl whenever."

Her sweet voice soothed the aches and blisters he'd worked up throughout the day.

"What are you doing here?" He took off his work gloves, grateful for the chill on his sweating hands.

"Randy said you called and were too busy to help tonight. You've been helping us out so much, I wanted to come to return the favor."

"You didn't have to do that."

"I wanted to. I came by at lunch, but you weren't here." She tucked her hands in her jacket pockets.

"If you would have called, I would have told you I had a load for the buyers' station."

"I did. And I texted."

Josh wiped his hands on his jeans. "Right. I did see that."

He felt like the backside of a donkey.

"What can I do to help?" She moved toward him.

"I'm finished for tonight. Sarah and the rest of them are waiting up at the house for our weekly supper. I've got to go."

He got two steps past her, his heart shrinking in his chest, and she said, "Josh, is there something the matter?"

"It's been a long day. I'll try to stop by tomorrow." And he left her standing there inside the barn.

Shoving the brim of his hat down, he marched to the house. Lord, he prayed, I'm such a fool. I don't deserve her. Nor does she deserve my behavior.

Turning on his heel, Josh marched back to the barn, where Alison had headed toward her car. "Alison, wait."

She glanced over at him in the dark. He could see the way the pole light outside the barn cast a golden hue over her pale face.

"Have you eaten?"

"No. I had to take on a client to fill in for a coworker who is sick. By the time I got back, I went straight to the barn. I sent Randy up to the house to check on Gramps and have a bite with him while I came here."

"Michael makes a mean chili. You're welcome to come inside and eat with us."

"Are you sure it would be okay? I don't want to impose."

Josh regretted making her feel that way. "I'd like you to."

Alison came over and took his arm. "Then, I'd like to very much."

As they walked, Josh struggled with asking Alison about seeing her with Jason. He decided for the moment he would enjoy her company as they walked to Sarah and Michael's house. He didn't know why he was letting it bother him so much.

"Is this where you live?" she asked.

Josh pointed across the darkness back down the lane. "My place is down there by the bridge. I stay in the old carriage house."

When they reached the porch, Sarah and Michael's oldest son, Ethan, opened the door for him. Seeing Alison, Ethan drew up his eight-year-old height to stand as tall as he could. "It's about time, Uncle Josh."

"Didn't see you down there helping me none," Josh said.

"Mom made me do homework."

Josh laid his hand on Ethan's shoulder. "Good. I hope you had lots of it."

Ethan stuck his dark head around Josh and glanced at Alison. "You bring a girl with you? I thought you said you didn't bring girls home?"

"This is my friend, Alison."

Josh didn't miss the frown on her face as she held out her hand to Ethan. "It's nice to meet you."

"This is Ethan." Josh ushered her inside as Ethan stood back and let them in.

"Kingsley. I'm Ethan Kingsley," Ethan corrected him.

"It's nice to meet you," Alison said.

Ethan directed his attention back to Josh. "Mom said not to wake the baby, or you got to watch him."

"Then you'd best not wake him." Josh shed his coat and held out his hand to help Alison, and she took hers off. Ethan beat him to take it, and Alison giggled.

"Show off," Josh grumbled.

Down the hall in the kitchen, he could hear Jenny's voice and Michael's, along with the others.

"Umm. It smells good in here," Alison said.

Josh led her to the kitchen. The conversation seemed to stop as he said, "Not as good as Thornton's, but it's good."

Michael coughed, and Cade stepped close to Jenny. Sarah gave him that hard glare, and Josh shrugged. "What? Just saying."

Alison had gone a bit peaked, and Jenny rushed over to her. "Hey, it's good to see you."

"Josh said it was okay for me to join you all."

"Absolutely." Michael Kingsley reached over and held out a bowl to her.

"You're always welcome. How is your grandfather?" Sarah asked, taking her gaze way from Josh.

Alison accepted the bowl of chili. Josh moved to get his own. Jenny and Cade moved and made space for Alison around the table, and Josh heard Alison telling them about Dwight's progress since coming home.

"There's been no luck in finding her horse?" Sarah whispered as Josh ladled chili in his bowl.

Josh shook his head.

Michael moved closer to Alison, while Ethan returned to his seat where a bowl of half-eaten chili remained.

"Are you going to be working with us, too?" Ethan asked.

"No. I have another job."

"Ethan," Michael warned.

Ethan shrugged. "What? She's having supper with us. No one comes and eats with us unless they help."

Michael pushed Ethan's bowl closer to him. "Eat your supper, kid, and be nice. Miss Vandergraft has a stable of her own."

"I do." Alison went on to say, "My family owns Windy Knoll, and I direct the Silver Stirrups Riding Club's program for seniors in the community. Well, Gramps did most while I worked, and Josh has been so kind coming over to help us, I came tonight to see if I could return the favor." She glanced over at him, a faint smile, and his treacherous heart betrayed him.

"Which she can't, because when someone does something nice for you, they're not expected to do it back in return." Josh pointed his fork, talking to Ethan.

"Thank you." Alison turned back to her chili, but Jenny narrowed her eyes at Josh. He could see the gears turning in his sister's head.

For the rest of the meal, Alison talked with Jenny and Sarah. He loved listening to Alison speak about the Silver Stirrups program for the seniors. He could see the joy radiating in her smile and her voice as she spoke.

"I really do appreciate you letting us borrow Josh for the trail rides on Wednesdays," Alison told them.

"You must have been desperate to make my brother the trail master." Jenny leaned back and rubbed her belly.

"He's doing a fine job. Gramps is worried he won't be able to get back in the saddle after having Josh fill in for him."

"It's my pleasure to help," Josh said.

"We'll have to get him another horse before your grandfather has to worry about going out on the trail again," Sarah said.

"I think Destiny might fit him well. She takes to the trail better than I figured," Josh said.

"I think it will be several months before Gramps gets on another horse. Even when he's healed, I think it will be hard for him."

Jenny rested her hand on Alison's arm. "Please know we've all been praying for you and your grandfather. You've had a tough time of late, and we're all here for you."

Alison blinked, and Josh cleared his throat, spying Ethan resting his head on his arms. "I think I should get going. I'm about as tuckered out as this guy here."

Sarah and Michael glanced in his direction, and Michael moved toward his son. "I've got him."

Cade moved behind Jenny, and they exchanged a look of pure love. It made Josh uncomfortable, as if he interrupted an intimate moment between them.

"I think we should head home, too, and put this baby to bed." He touched Jenny's belly, and she scowled at him.

"Careful, she gets grumpy when she's tired," Josh warned.

"Don't I know it." Cade grinned down at his wife, holding the chair as Jenny held out her hand, and Josh pulled his sister to her feet.

"Just for that, I'm making you stay up at night with this one." She grinned and patted her well-rounded stomach.

Alison rose, too. "Do you need any help cleaning up?"

Sarah began to clean off the table. "No. Michael will get Ethan settled, and I've got this, but thank you for offering."

"Thank you for supper."

Josh followed Alison, who followed Jenny and Cade down the hall.

"Good night," Sarah called.

Chapter Eleven

Josh walked Alison to her car. "I can give you a ride to your place."

"I've got to take my truck to my place, so it's out of Cade's way in the morning."

Alison swallowed hard. She couldn't put her finger on it, but something didn't feel right between them.

"Will I see you tomorrow?"

"I can't."

She tried to swallow down her disappointment. "Sunday?" She ran her schedule through her head, and she could put Jason off until later on Sunday.

"I'm going to my church on Sunday. My mom is expecting me for dinner."

She noticed he hadn't included her in those plans. She tried to tell herself it was for the best. It wasn't as if they had been back together for long. She shouldn't expect to see his parents so soon again, but she couldn't help the disappointment. "So I'll see you when I see you?"

"That's about it."

Under the gleam of the pole light, Alison stepped up and wrapped her arms around him. Josh stiffened, and she pulled back from hugging him. "Call me when you're able."

She got in her car, her stomach more upset by his lack of returning her affection than the hot chili she consumed. Her heart beat fast as she thought about not seeing him again and having to go out with Jason again.

Alison bound back out of the car. "Josh."

He turned, halfway to his truck.

"You're not gonna call me, are you?"

His head hung low, and he put his hand up to fix his hat. "Do you want me to call you?"

She took a deep breath. "I do."

Josh started walking toward his truck.

"Josh Anderson, don't you walk away from me again."

That stopped him. Josh spun on his heel and marched back to her. "Does this look like I'm walking away?"

He grabbed her and kissed her. Shocked and delighted by his curt advance, Alison clung to him and kissed him back. She had to hold onto her car door when he let her go to keep from tumbling.

"I saw you at Thornton's."

"I'm sorry." Of all the places and the time, she should have known in a town like Shelbyville if Josh hadn't seen her, then someone else would, and the gossip vine could get long in a town this size.

"Sorry I saw you or sorry I saw you with him?" Josh's voice grew harsh.

"Are you jealous?" It was a side of him she hadn't ever seen before. Alison tilted her head. "You are."

"A man's got a right to be upset when the woman he's dating is out with her ex."

Susan Lower

A little part of her wished he'd get jealous more often by the way he kissed her. Wrong, to think that, she couldn't help the little zings still tickling her belly from his lips crushing against hers.

"I'm not dating Jason. You're the one I'm seeing. The only one I want to see." She couldn't help thinking this sounded more like something they'd say back in high school.

Josh stuffed his hands in his pockets, a habit she noticed he often did. "It seemed more than friendly."

She tried to think of what Josh might have seen. "It was friends. A couple of drinks with Chelsea and Sean. We've known them for years," she explained.

"When I saw you with him, I thought you decided to go back to him. Not like I don't deserve it." Josh took her hands in his.

"Stop. You could have come in and said hello." Part of her wished he would have. Jason had glued his hand to her back and kept her close the entire time.

While she enjoyed seeing Chelsea again, she realized in the time she parted from Jason how much different their values were from each other. Jason had more than enough to drink. She almost called a cab to take her home. She couldn't afford the cab fare, and Jason insisted he pick her up and take her home.

She shivered, remembering how he leaned in and demanded a kiss goodnight. She gave him a peck on the cheek. She was thankful Gramps waited up for her, and Jason let her go because of it.

"No, I couldn't. Bars aren't my thing, and I'll be honest, it surprised me to see you there."

Neither were they hers, but Jason insisted, and Thornton's was a family tavern that served food in the back.

"But you were there," she said.

"Getting wings and fries to surprise you."

"Oh." Alison stepped closer to him, wanting him to hold her, warm her, and comfort her that things between them would always be right. "I do like their wings. Jason said if I went with him, he'd help me find Gus."

"Isn't my help enough?" Josh sounded hurt.

"Of course." Alison squeezed his hand. "I can't stand not knowing where Gus is. The police have had no more leads, and after Gramps had to say goodbye to Mistress ..." She got choked up.

She shook her head, trying to keep the tears from falling. She pushed the sob back down her throat, too late. Josh slid his hand along her cheek. "What did he tell you?"

She sniffled. "Nothing. Jason wouldn't tell me anything after I went out with him." She bit her lip, realizing how it might sound.

"Ali, I don't want you seeing him. He lied to you to get you to go out with him."

"Jason doesn't lie. Whatever he knows, he won't tell me until he's ready." Alison leaned into Josh. God knew all the things she'd been through and what lay on her heart. How could she explain all the things to Josh of what the last several years had been like with Jason?

"If he knows anything at all." Josh gathered her in his arms as she shivered again. "Listen. I know guys like him. They string girls along until they get what they want. My dad's got a friend he went to school with that works in the police department. I'll ask him to see what he says about the case. Was Jason even a suspect?"

"Jason's allergic to horses. He never steps foot in the stables. He couldn't. He wouldn't be able to breathe with the hay and the horses."

"Hmmm ..." Josh kissed the top of her head.

"What?"

"It's late. I'll follow you out the lane until I get to my place. Text me, so I know you're home safe."

They went from awkward, to cozy, to hash things out, to him sending her off. She let him open the door and help her into the driver seat again. "You'll call me."

"As soon as I talk to my dad on Sunday." He gave her another quick peck on the cheek.

True to his word, Josh followed her down the lane until he turned off to the carriage house on the other side of the bridge. Once she got home, she found Gramps asleep in his chair and an old black-and-white western playing on the television. She cleaned up the dirty dishes beside him and placed a blanket over him. She left the TV on in case he woke when she turned off the background noise.

Inside her room, she texted Josh.

I'm home.

How is Gramps?

Asleep.

Me too. Sweet dreams.

She almost texted back, but she knew he must be tired. She thanked God Josh hadn't walked away from her tonight. He had no idea how much of her heart he would have taken with him this time. And she prayed God would help her figure out what to do about Jason and find Gus. Could it be she needed to let him go? And if she did, she prayed wherever her beloved horse was, that he was being cared for properly.

Alison remembered the plants from Mrs. Crawford and made sure to put them inside to avoid the frost and cold of the night. In a few days, it would be March, which meant Alison would have to make some decisions about work and keeping up with Windy Knoll and the Silver Stirrups Riding Club. One day without Josh had made her realize how very much she needed an extra hand if she was to keep up with her clients or give them up ... and which ones?

At least she had some time to decide, and she planned to ask Gramps for advice in the morning.

The last person Alison expected to see in the barn before seven stood holding coffee with a huge grin. He had muck on his boots and his jacket slung over a hook by the door. His stained hoodie had the logo for a feed mill not far from them.

While she loved his cowboy hat on Sundays, she'd come to like his worn ball cap more. It gave him this attractive country boy look that made her go all warm inside.

"It's early."

Josh scoffed. "Honey, I've been up for a few hours now. You're the sleepy head."

Alison took the coffee. She could smell the dark roast coming from the lounge area expanded in the corner of the barn, where Gramps had torn out some old stalls to make room for people to congregate before and after rides.

"How did you know I'd want coffee?" she asked.

"I didn't. I got that for me. But I'm a nice guy, so I'll share." He winked and went to grab another cup. As he poured another mug, she sipped the one he handed her.

"The feeding is done. I put Destiny in Mistress's old stall. Not many to choose from, but I needed a place to keep her this week. Otherwise, I wouldn't have a horse for Wednesday's ride. I think Joe McIntyre has taken a shine to her and asked if he could saddle her up on Saturday."

"What about you? Hasn't she become your horse? You ride her an awful lot." Alison moved down the aisle, unsure how she felt about seeing another horse in Mistress's stall. She expected to get angry or upset, and a little piece of her ached for the horse that wouldn't ever stand in this stall again. But somehow seeing the horse there was as if the leggy mare belonged. Maybe she should give the horse a chance.

Maddy Pierce had grown attached to Texas, and maybe Destiny had a place here at Windy Knoll as well.

"I don't mind not having my own. There are plenty at the rescue needing attention."

Sarah had mentioned in the winter they had more horses needing shelter and proper care beyond the other months. People neglected all kinds of pets, but it always broke Alison's heart to think someone would neglect or abuse a horse. It made her feel bad, too, that Josh came out to her barn to feed horses when he had so much to do at Silver Wind.

She'd seen the way he worked with Destiny. Even though his words said he wouldn't mind seeing Destiny with someone else, she wasn't blind. She'd have to speak with Gramps and add it to her prayers.

"You didn't have to come out here this morning. I can get the feeding done before I start on my visits for the day."

"Then I wouldn't get to see you." Josh leaned back against the wall. That sly grin of his and dancing light in his eyes would make any girl's heart melt. It most certainly had its effects on her.

"I was doing some thinking last night," she confessed. "I've been praying about it, and with the new month gonna start, Gramps hurt, and you — I think I'm going to request fewer clients during the day."

Josh put down his coffee on the window seal nearby. "Can you do that?"

"I've taken on quite a number of clients through the years, and there are never enough of us on staff, it seems, for all the needs."

"That's not what I meant. Can you afford it?"

Alison had thought about that, too. Jason always pushed her to work and take extra people. Work now, retire early had been his drive. He hardly spent a dollar on things if he could get away with it. He always said he'd need it when he got older. And Alison had put back a small sum since Jason would frown on her spending it for something he deemed frivolous.

"I think so. I've been working and not spending so I can afford to cut a few hours for a few months while Gramps recovers and take care of the farm and give more attention to the riding club."

"I'll help you any way I can," Josh said.

"It's not the money," Alison assured him, but she loved him nonetheless. It made her heart skip a beat and her hands get tingly. "Gramps has got his pension, and the Silver Stirrups members pay to board their horses here. We were talking about expanding the barn before Gramps's accident."

"I have to haul tonight and work at the auction. I won't be able to stop by and help. Cade has his hands full with training the rescue horses, and Sarah's got her hands full with the baby and rescue business."

"Randy will be coming by. He can help, and I'll take care of the rest."

Josh moved over, kissed her square on the lips, and it wouldn't ever get old, Alison thought, taking hold of his jacket and leaning into more of his kiss.

It ended too short. No matter: they both lost track of time, and Alison's phone rang from inside her jeans pocket.

Her stomach soured, seeing Jason's number pop up, but she answered anyway.

"Hey, beautiful."

Josh stiffened next to her, but she held on to him.

"Good morning, Jason." She glanced up at Josh, his eyes narrowed.

"Hey, beautiful, I'm packing extra for lunch today. Meet me at the park at noon."

"Noon?" She didn't take her eyes from Josh. Her fingers touched her lips.

"That's what I said."

"I don't know."

Josh crossed his arms.

"Don't, Alison. Not if you want me to help you get Gus back," Jason's voice cracked over the phone. He must be on his drive to work for the reception to crackle.

Josh shook his head.

"I can't."

"Not even for Gus?" Jason sounded disbelieving.

Alison bit her lip. Her heart seemed too small in her chest. "Another time?"

"Noon," Jason said.

"I'm with a client."

Jason made an agitated sound in his voice. "Supper."

"Not unless you want to eat after nine," she told him.

Josh's expression darkened.

"Tomorrow," Jason challenged.

"You're welcome to come over and have supper with Gramps and me," Alison said to Josh. "You too."

"You who?" Jason swore, and Alison figured it was from traffic and not her, but she couldn't tell. All she could see was the disappointment in Josh's eyes.

"Josh," she said, "you know the guy I'm seeing." In more ways than one.

"Tell your boyfriend to stay at home. This is between us. If you know what is good for you, you'll break up with him and tell him about us."

"Us?" she whispered.

Josh took the phone from her. "Listen, man. Do you know where the horse is? Be the good guy and save the day by telling the police so they can return it and catch the thief. Either way, Ali is with me."

Josh handed the phone back.

"What did he say?"

"He hung up." Josh fixed his hat. "That's why I came here this morning. I wanted to tell you I've been thinking about what you said last night."

Behind her, one of the horses knocked its bucket, and she could hear the water splashing and the other sounds of horses pulling hay through their racks.

"Josh, I want my horse back."

"You think playing games with your ex rather than trusting me and trusting the police will find Gus? You're not the person I thought you were."

"I don't know what else to do," Alison confessed.

"Trust me." Josh took her face in his hands. "Let the police do their job. I told you I'd talk to my dad and his friend on the force. Come with me on Sunday to church. You can meet my parents. Don't let this jerk pull you along."

Alison took a deep breath. "Okay. We'll do this your way."

He kissed her, and Alison lost all other doubts.

Chapter Twelve

On Sunday, a cold front swept over the county, and while the snow had melted days ago, the bitter chill of the wind could slice through a man's flesh and freeze his blood in minutes.

Thankful to spend time in church with Alison at his side, Josh left his reservations in the hands of the Lord. Jenny and Cade missed service and promised to meet at their parents' later for Sunday dinner. Josh could hear the excitement in his mother's voice when he called and let her know he was bringing a guest after church.

He wondered if his mother would remember Alison. Of course, she did. Mary Anderson never forgot a face. Alison brought along a batch of cookies she'd baked, and his mother set them aside for coffee afterward. He'd never been so relieved to see his sister and Cade in his life as Josh didn't bother knocking and escorted Alison into the house. "Mom. We're here."

Mary came out of the kitchen, her cheeks plump and flushed with preparing their meal. Her eyes got all glistening like she wanted to cry. He tried hard not to roll his eyes. He stepped away from Alison and gave his mother a peck on the cheek. "It's dinner, Mom. I haven't asked her to marry me."

His mother nodded and patted his arm. "It's good to see you. Jenny said you've been busy and helping a friend. This must be your friend." His mom leaned around him to smile at Alison. "I'm Mary, Josh's mother."

"I remember," Alison said.

Mary's face brightened. "Oh, good." She waved them through the doorway. "Come in. Come in out of the cold."

Alison made sure to close the door, and from there, his mother swept her up in a hug. Josh caught the cookies before they fell.

"Oh my!" Alison giggled, then hugged his mother in return. "Thank you for having me, Mrs. Anderson."

"Call me Mary. It's been too long, Ali, dear." A timer went off, and Mary jerked back. "That'll be dinner. Right on time."

She hurried away, and Josh helped Alison with the cookies, sneaking one as he put them down in the dining room. Cade gave him a look, and he passed a cookie to Josh while Jenny waddled into the kitchen with their mother.

A few moments later, as he stood with his arm around Alison, Josh's father, Bill, walked out with a large pot of mashed potatoes. "Your mother said not to touch these while she gets the rest."

"Dad, you remember Alison?"

"Of course. She is the girl you said needs help to find her horse." Bill Anderson was a stout man, with a head of dark rust hair and silver sideburns. He looked surprised as Josh's mother had gone all weepy for a second, but Bill Anderson was known for keeping a level head. He nodded at Alison. "Nice to see you again."

"You have a lovely home." Alison took the seat Josh offered her. Mary came in, carrying a roaster with meatloaf. Too late, Josh should have thought to warn Alison about his mother's meatloaf. He could only hope Jenny hadn't lied when she said his mother's cooking had gotten better with her age. Jenny came in with steaming green beans, and Cade moved to take them from her.

"That leg bothering you again?" Mary asked Cade.

"It's the weather. My hip gets stiff with the cold," Cade said.

Jenny eased down in a chair near him and placed her hand on his leg. "He's too stubborn to take it easy for a few days." Then she rolled her eyes and said, "Men."

All the women laughed, and Bill cleared his throat. "Let's say grace before the food gets cold."

Josh glanced over at Alison, and he gave her a wink to make her smile. He took Alison's hand, and she reached and took his father's. They held hands for grace, and while Bill said the blessing over the food, Josh said a little prayer of his own.

"You get any bigger, and you won't be able to reach the table." Josh slid the mashed potatoes closer to him as Jenny reached for them. He did it on purpose, and she scowled at him.

Cade shook his head and stabbed a piece of meatloaf. Alison took a piece of bread and buttered it while she waited for Josh to offer her potatoes while Bill passed the green beans.

"It won't be much longer," Mary beamed, gazing over at Jenny, all dreamy for a woman who would soon become a grandmother.

"You just wait," Jenny said to him, getting her hands on the mashed potatoes after Cade patiently waited for a turn. "I hope one day you get the twins."

"It skips a generation, doesn't it?" Alison asked.

"You know about twins?" Mary asked.

Alison finished chewing the bit of meatloaf she stuck in her mouth. "One of my clients had triplet grandsons."

"Would that be Barbara Blandford?" Mary asked.

"Didn't she pass last year?" his father said.

Alison made a face. Josh couldn't be sure if it was from his mother's over-salty meatloaf or the mention of someone passing.

"She did. And it was Barbara. I visited her for a few months before she died," Alison said.

Josh spoke up before his mother could ask and said, "Alison's a home visit person for the elderly."

"I provide support for those at home."

"Have you always worked with the elderly?" Jenny asked.

"No. I started with special needs kids in schools, but when my Gram got sick, I switched to helping her and have since been helping the senior community."

"And now, your grandfather. I'm so sorry to have heard of his accident. We've been praying for him. Maddy Pierce attends our church and said about the trail master of her riding club getting injured. It wasn't until Jenny said Josh was helping you out at Windy Knoll that I put two and two together."

That wasn't all his mother had put together. He recognized that look in her eye, and between his mother and Jenny, the two of them were hearing wedding bells. Well, he'd make them wait because he was sure he and Alison weren't at that stage yet. He wanted to be certain Alison felt the same way about him.

"I don't know what we would have done without Josh these past weeks. The seniors in the riding club have been making sure we don't run out of meals, but having an extra set of hands at the barn has been a godsend. Without Josh leading the trail rides every week, I don't know what we would have done."

"You could lead them," Jenny said, taking another heaping spoonful of mashed potatoes.

"I can't." Alison's voice wavered. "I don't have a horse, and neither does Gramps, anymore."

Cade shifted in his seat, and a moment later, Jenny put down the next spoonful of potatoes. She gave Cade a dark scowl, and Josh shook his head. "Geez, Jenny."

"I was just saying."

"You'd better keep eating." Cade picked up her spoon for her and directed it back to her mouth.

"How do you go on the trail rides without a horse?" their mother asked, innocently.

"Mary," Bill spoke up, pushing his finished plate away. While everyone talked, he had eaten. "Your horse is the one Josh told me about? The one that got stolen?"

Alison nodded, her eyes going down to the green beans she pushed on the plate.

"Oh my, that was your horse? I'm so sorry," Mary said.

"We're going to find him." Josh leaned into Alison, and she glanced over at him. That little peek from those beautiful eyes sent his head spinning. He gripped his water glass to gain balance.

"Connor Dixon will be coming over in about an hour or so. I promised him coffee and dessert, but he said he's happy to help. He didn't think he could do much. He said the case had been investigated, and with only one suspect who seems on the up and up. Without any other evidence, it's like finding a needle in a haystack."

"He's probably right," Cade said. "We had horses go missing from time to time on the circuit. Tats in horses' lips can be changed, and papers made to look like the real ones. Most horses don't have that or even a brand these days. Unless the horse has special coloring and it's national news, I don't want to hurt your feelings, but you might not see your horse again."

Alison put down her fork and slipped her hands under the table to her lap. "I know. I am having trouble getting over someone wanting to steal him. It's not like he's worth a lot, I mean for money. He's special to me. I've had him for so long, and I can't think why anyone would take a horse from the stables."

"Don't you lock up at night?" Jenny hurried and put more food in her mouth.

"We have security cameras, and in the warm weather, we sometimes leave the horses out all night."

"We've had a flyer up at the rescue, and I know Sarah has asked around," Cade said.

"Connor seemed to think it was someone who knew their way around the place. There were plenty of horses they could have taken, but they only took one. As you said, there are other horses there that might be worth more than yours if they were looking to steal to make money," Bill tapped on his chin.

"Well, let's wait for Connor, and you all can talk about this when he comes." Mary directed the conversation away from Alison's stolen horse to the upcoming arrival of Mary's first grandchild.

That seemed to relax Alison a bit. Josh slid his hand under the table and held her hand. Later, as Alison offered to help his mom clean up in the kitchen, and Cade made Jenny put her feet up in her dad's recliner in the living room, Josh answered the door when Connor arrived.

They took their discussion to the dining room with coffee and slices of warm apple pie and delicious snickerdoodles from Alison.

Hearing the voices, Alison came to join them. Cade warned Jenny not to get up as he left the room to join their discussion. He took her pie and made her settle for black tea without the caffeine. "She already keeps me up all night," he grumbled.

Bill smirked and gave Connor a knowing glance among men who were married with children. Alison sat closest to Connor, and Josh could see the disappointment sag in her shoulders as Connor told her the same thing Josh's dad had said earlier.

"Unless there's a new suspect or the horse appears, and someone can prove it's yours, there's not much else to do."

"There was nothing on the surveillance cameras?" Cade asked.

Alison shook her head. "Randy, but he's always there. He's a close friend of Gramps who helps us in the barn. It gets him out since he lives alone with his dog."

"He's not a member of the riding club?" Bill asked.

"Honorary, I guess you could say. Randy doesn't ride. He says it's because of his bad knees. Truth be told, I think he's just afraid of falling off. I once heard Gramps talking about a bad experience Randy had on a horse when he was younger."

"But he helps at the barn? You pay him?" Connor asked.

"It's volunteer. The Silver Stirrups Riding Club is a nonprofit. We only charge what it costs to upkeep the stable and for the horses to stay there, but we're going to have to hire someone to run the barn and oversee things soon. Some of the members have offered to do what they can, but not many of them can do the heavy lifting or always get out in the weather. Plus, Randy isn't going to be able to keep up with a full barn, and Gramps can't, either."

"You have me," Josh said.

Mary snorted, stepping into the dining room. "Son, you have so many jobs now, you're not going to be able to keep up with them."

"She's right." Cade reached for a cookie. "You've got too many things on your plate as it is."

"What?" Josh made a pfff sound. "Hauling is slow in the winter. You've got the rescue side, and I've got the clinic. Michael needs to hire a regular assistant instead of a stable hand for his runs."

"What about auctions?" Alison asked. "You said you couldn't help the other day. You had too much going on."

"And we were hoping you helping Michael at the clinic would inspire you," Mary added.

Josh glanced between all of them. How had they gone from trying to help Alison find her missing horse to his job situation? And all this talk had made Alison's lips turn down in a frown that he didn't like seeing.

"How are you gonna ever support a family without a steady job?"

And there it was. The elephant that always lingered in the room whenever Josh came to visit with his parents. It didn't matter that he had a business of his own or that he was a few years shy of thirty. He got up and cleared away his plate. "Then it's a good thing by you all's account I don't have a family."

Alison stared at him, her jaw a little slack. He supposed he spoke out of turn, and it wasn't even Jenny who'd gotten under his skin this time.

"Listen. I've got a job. I understand you all don't see it that way, but hauling is my business. It isn't prestigious, and it doesn't come with health insurance and a retirement package, but it's what I like to do. I couldn't work in an office or a factory. I need to be on the move, and I like helping people. I like helping at Windy Knoll as much as I'm a part of the rescue and working at the clinic. I'm the 'go-to' guy, and I wish you all could accept that."

Josh headed for the kitchen, leaving his parents staring slack-jawed as he exited. Inside the kitchen, the quiet that stretched from the other room unnerved him. He kicked the dishwasher shut after putting his plate inside and reached for the back door as Jenny waddled inside. "If you want to go, Cade and I can see Alison home."

She said it like a whisper so the others couldn't hear her. Josh leaned back against the counter, running his hands through his hair. "Who says I'm going anywhere without Alison?"

Jenny grimaced and rubbed her stomach. "They mean well. They worry."

"They have nothing to worry about."

"Even with your track record?" Jenny's brow rose.

Josh crossed his arms. He should have known Cade would tell Jenny, and she would spread his troubled past to his parents. In another year, he'd have Cade paid back, and his hauling income would suffice to provide for his needs. But would they be enough for a family? His father's question bothered him. Would Alison want to marry him if she knew the debts he had and how he got them? Would she care he was paying them off and working hard to set things right in his life?

"If you don't stop thinking so hard, bro, you're going to hurt yourself," Jenny said.

"I wouldn't have to if you'd stop thinking you have any right to interfere with other people's lives." And he said it, and he hurt her.

Cade stepped into the kitchen with his limp more pronounced than usual. Big tears sprung from Jenny's eyes.

"What's going on?" Cade asked.

Jenny turned and buried her face in Cade's chest as his arms came around her.

"What have you told my parents? I thought we had an agreement."

Cade seemed taken aback. He glanced down at Jenny. "We. Do."

Jenny turned her head away, and Josh couldn't help the tick of his jaw. "We might, but that didn't stop you from telling her."

"She's my wife."

"You forget she's my meddling sister."

Jenny sniffled. "I just want you to be happy."

"By telling Mom and Dad my business? Is that any way to help?"

"Jenny." Cade gently pulled Jenny from him. "Please tell me you didn't."

Jenny glanced between Josh and Cade. More tears slid down her cheeks.

Mary stepped into the kitchen. "We're your parents, Josh. We have a right to know what's going on in your life. How else can we help you and pray for you?"

Josh heard enough. He pushed past his mother and into the dining room. Alison saw him and said to his father and Connor, "I think that's my cue that we're leaving. It is so kind of you to help me. I'll keep this and give you a call." She held a small business card in her hand. "Thank you for dinner," she told his father and glanced behind him at her mother.

"You don't have to go," Mary said.

"Alison needs to get back to her grandfather." Josh grabbed their coats and rushed her out before his parents tried to crowd them with hugs. Outside in the truck, he took a deep breath and placed the key in the ignition.

117

Chapter Thirteen

Alison gave Josh some time as he backed out of his parents' driveway, and they took the back roads home. Outside, the world appeared like a painting with blue skies and yellow-green grasses except for the cold that sent a person huddling close to the heater. Alison huddled in her jacket and waited for the truck heat to blow hot air.

Josh grimaced, gave it a slam of his fist on the dash, and a few moments later, a small trickle of warm air blew from the vents.

As the inside of the cab started to warm up, he said, "Thanks."

"Is it always like that when you visit your parents?" Not one for prying, she hoped he would open up and trust her enough to share. "It seemed like it was going to get intense in there."

Her conversation with Connor had paused several times as if the men in the room with her waited for a bomb to go off or something to crash. Mary had seemed nervous, shuffling on her feet, and finally turned to investigate the muffled voices in the kitchen.

"As you can tell, my parents aren't keen on my choice of professions."

"I understand. Parents always seem to want the best for their children. Mine tried to get me to move with them when my dad took a new job in

Georgia. Scott went along with them, but I had my life here and wanted to stay."

"There's more to it than that."

She waited to see if he would tell her and fought with the temptation to prompt him along. Seeing the way he interacted with his family, it must have been tense for him to bring her to meet his parents and for him to ask for help from his dad for her to speak with Connor.

She had no more hope now as she did before today on getting her beloved horse back. Her only lead right now was Jason.

She knew not all families had the same kind of relationships as she had with her parents, and she liked to tease her younger brother. She also missed him more than she thought she would. Every week she looked forward to talking with her mom and keeping in touch.

Josh watched the road as he drove. His hands clamped on the steering wheel. She decided to try and ease the tension emulating from him.

"Your sister seems like she's pretty far along. When is she due?"

"End of the month."

"Not long then. Does Jenny know what she is having?"

Josh's fingers relaxed. "Cade would have like to have known, but Jenny wanted it to be a surprise, and Jenny always gets her way."

The bitterness in his voice hadn't escaped her attention. "I've heard having a baby can mean enduring a bit of pain. I think I agree with your sister. I'd want the surprise. You know, after going through the labor of having that one thing to motivate you through delivery to have to find out."

Josh glanced over at her as he slowed at a light in town. "You would?"

"Well, yeah." Alison had thought about it a few times on the occasion when she let her mind wander about having kids of her own. With all the technologies they have now compared to her grandmother's or her mother's time. She'd imagined having boys or girls and which one came first, but in the long run, God knew who her child would be and who would father them. Every time she considered accepting Jason's proposal, she couldn't imagine having children with him.

Josh, on the other hand, she could see strawberry blond-haired babies with big blue eyes and a smattering of freckles when they got older. Oh yes, indeed, she could imagine a family with Josh.

Then she stopped herself from letting her mind wander even further. They were dating. And they hadn't been together that long for her think of Josh as the father of her children. He hadn't even talked of love, let alone marriage!

"What about you?" Alison watched him relax more.

"I'd go with whatever my wife wanted."

She heard the truth in his voice. "Kids or no kids?"

"Don't matter to me. I want my wife to be happy." Josh stole a glance at her, and Alison's cheeks went from cold to hot fast.

"You still want to date me if I tell you I want as many as God will give me?"

She laughed at the incredulous look on his face.

Josh turned his gaze back on the road. Then as time stretched and Alison ceased laughing, he said, "I'd date you no matter what." His soft confession turned her insides to mush. He took her hand, brought it to his lips, and gave her a wink while the truck came to a halt at the next stop sign.

Alison slid as close as she could in the truck while keeping her seatbelt on.

"Did Connor say he could help you much more after I went into the kitchen?"

"No." Oddly, she was okay with that.

"I'm sorry."

"It's not your fault." They would find Gus when the timing was right. And maybe she wouldn't ever see Gus again, but she had faith. She put her horse in God's hands, and her relationship with Josh.

Down the lane, at Windy Knoll's barn, Alison spotted Jason's vehicle by the barn, parked alongside Randy's. "What is he doing here?"

Josh pulled up and parked by the barn instead of going to the house.

"I thought you told me he didn't like animals."

"He's allergic to them."

Alison didn't wait for Josh to come around and get the door. She was out of the truck and marching toward the barn. Jason never went into the barn. Not even when they were together. He would come outside to the fields and the riding ring where the air wasn't polluted with horsehair or dander. An awful feeling twisted in her gut.

A few strides from the door, Jason walked out from around the side of the barn, followed by Randy. "There she is." Jason put on a broad grin.

Josh stepped up behind Alison. "What's up?"

"He came looking for you. I tried to tell him you weren't here," Randy said.

"What are you doing here?" Alison crossed her arms.

"I haven't seen you all week, and you weren't at church today, so I dropped by to check on you. I didn't know if something happened with Gramps."

Alison glanced at the house, a moment of panic kicking her in the gut.

"Dwight's napping in his chair. We had lunch an hour ago," Randy huffed, moving toward his truck. "I took care of that broken gate, and Jason gave me a hand, seeing no one else was around."

Josh held his voice tight. "It could have waited until Monday. There shouldn't be any horses out today or need to use that gate."

"Dwight wanted it taken care of."

"I never knew you to be handy with tools," Alison said.

Jason moved closer, trying to put himself between her and Josh, but Josh pulled her closer against him. "Just because you haven't seen me doesn't mean I can't."

"I'd better check that gate before I go," Josh said.

"I'll go with you." Alison went to see the gate. Randy walked away. "I've been away from the house too long. I can't be here tomorrow."

Alison took a deep breath and tried to decide how best to handle having to stand between the man she once thought she would love forever and the one who had no idea she loved him.

"I've got it, old man," Josh said.

Randy waved, not bothering to look back or react.

Alison punched him in the arm.

"What?" Josh rubbed his arm. "He's the one always saying he's too old to do this kind of stuff anymore."

"Alison, I was about to go up and see Gramps. Come with me?" Jason started walking toward the house.

Not thinking, she started to follow him until Josh grabbed hold of her hand. "It'll be okay."

She gave him a peck on the cheek and walked off before she lost her nerve. Halfway to the house, Jason slowed his step, and she fell in alongside him. "I don't know what you see in that dead weight."

"It's not your business." Alison lengthened her stride, wanting to get to the house and get this visit over. She'd gone from one family's drama to the pit of her own. Gramps would handle Jason. He could be firm-handed when the situation called for it. And right now, it called for it. She couldn't keep letting Jason try to control her again.

"Alison, I love you. How could it not be my business? I know you wanted a break. I get it. But I can't stand by and watch you being taken advantage of."

"The only one taking advantage of me, Jason, I feel is you. Why else won't you tell me what you think you know that would help me find Gus?"

Jason rushed up the porch stairs ahead of her and stood in her way. "Gus is safe, Alison. Or at least he's in better hands wherever he's at than with that hustler you're seeing."

"Josh isn't a hustler." Alison stepped around him, but Jason wouldn't let her get to the door without blocking her from opening the screen door.

"Alison," Jason sighed dramatically. So like Jason. Alison tried to hold her patience. "I didn't want to tell you this, but I suppose it is the only way."

"Whatever you have to say, you can do it inside with Gramps and me when Josh comes to join us." Her toes had started to get cold in the dress boots she put on this morning for church. She had wanted to impress Josh's parents.

"You want Gramps to hear all this? Won't the stress cause a relapse or something?"

Alison could see he wanted to tell her and wasn't going to let her go inside until he did. "Fine. Tell me what it is you think is so bad about Josh. But then, you have to tell me what you know about Gus's disappearance."

Jason's mouth twitched, and his eyes lit with a gleam Alison hadn't seen since he tried to surprise her on her twenty-first birthday.

"That's the thing, beautiful. I think your new boyfriend was in on it."

Cold filled Alison's lungs. She glanced over to where Josh had disappeared into the barn, her mind listening to Jason as her heart raced with his words.

"You shouldn't accuse people of things you don't have proof for." She notched her chin and looked Jason square in the eye.

He didn't back down. His expression softened, his eyes a little bigger at her challenging him. "Alison, the guy's a dirty swindler. He doesn't care what he hauls or for whom as long as he gets paid. Ask Randy, he'll tell you."

Alison tried to hold down the anger building inside her. "You're trying to twist this into something to make Josh look bad. I'm disappointed in you. I thought you were a bigger man than this."

Alison tried again to open the door.

"I'm telling you. Ask around. I can give you the name of a detective if you want. Josh Anderson makes bets at the horse races, and he's been known to smuggle horses across state lines for the right price."

"Of course he does. It's his business to haul livestock."

"That's not what I mean." Jason's voice rose. "Alison, listen to me!"

"I don't need to hear another word," she said.

"Neither do I."

Alison jolted at the sound of Gramps's voice. He stood there with the door open. "You all are interrupting John Wayne's BBQ on television, and my granddaughter's lips are turning blue. Is that any way to treat a woman?"

Jason averted his eyes. "No, sir."

Alison took a moment and opened the screen door and went inside.

"I'd invite you inside, but I don't think that would be wise." Gramps started to shut the door.

"I'll call you later." Jason turned and strode off the porch.

Inside, Alison found it easier to breathe, and the sudden warmth of the house made her start to sweat. She pulled off her jacket and went about kicking off her boots.

"Want to tell me what all he said to get you upset?" Gramps moved slow, shuffling to get back to his chair and ease down in it.

"He implied Josh had something to do with Gus disappearing and said he gambles at the horse races." Alison sank on the couch nearest to Gramps's chair. She wrung her hands together, trying to warm them.

"You have a good time after church?" Gramps leaned back in his chair and put the footrest up.

She hadn't expected his nonchalant attitude over her encounter with Jason. She was still wondering what he was doing outside with Randy. Neither one of them would have had any purpose out there, especially Randy, on such a cold day.

"You meet the parents?"

Gramps question pulled her away from her own. "Yes. They're nice people."

"How was the sermon this morning?" Gramps laid his hand on the old Bible by his chair. He'd asked her to put it there this morning.

"It was about God putting the right people in certain places for the times to come."

She remembered thinking God had brought Josh to her when she needed him. She wouldn't let Jason's accusations settle any deeper. She'd been wrong not to be upfront with Josh when she went out with Jason, and he'd seen her. He gave her a chance to explain, and she owed him the same. Her heart demanded it.

"That's a good story." Gramps wiggled a little, and Alison took the hint that Gramps would soon be asleep again. She moved closer and fixed his lap quilt back around his hips and legs.

"Gramps?" She bit her lip, chewing on the thought for a second longer.

"Whatever it is, Ali girl, you can ask." His voice sounded tired.

"Do you think what Jason said has any weight?"

"It's not what I think that matters. Do I think your new young man has made mistakes? I'd be disappointed if he didn't. I also think that your history with Jason is blurring your heart, and he's not much of a man to try manipulating a girl's emotions."

"That's why I couldn't marry him," Alison confessed.

"I know." Gramps kept his eyes on the old John Wayne movie. "You haven't come this far, to go back now. Desperate men will do desperate things when they're about to lose what they set out to claim."

Alison covered her mouth, trying not to giggle. Gramps deepened his voice and sounded like a copycat of John Wayne. She hadn't heard him do that in a long time.

"Desperate enough to take a girl's horse?" Alison murmured.

"Why don't you ask him?"

"Who?"

"The young feller who's driving away down the lane."

Alison got up and looked out the window. Josh's truck headed down the lane. A second later, her phone chimed, and she checked the text.

Gate is good.

Thank you.

Are we good?

Alison held the phone. Behind her, a soft snore came from Gramps. She reread the text, believing they had no reason not to be. She texted.

Good.

See you in the morning?

Bright and early.

Chapter Fourteen

Josh quickly learned to time his escape after delivering a horse to the stables at Cottonwood Acres. The owner's daughter, Rachel Demoss, had a way of keeping him cornered for at least an hour since he made the mistake of driving her home one night from a stakes race a few years back. She'd drank her losses in fear of what her father would say when he found out she'd gambled one of their better mares and lost.

Luckily, Josh was able to make a trade deal and get the horse back before Rachel had to tell her father. It took a few swaps and several favors to pull it all off.

Rachel had been grateful, too grateful for a girl a few years younger than Josh. She had been hinting for him to take her out ever since.

"There's a race Friday night down at Bowman's field. You going?"

Josh latched the back gate of his trailer and secured the door. "Nope."

"Haven't seen you around in a while. People have been asking about you."

By "people," he assumed she meant one of the bookies and the old crowd he used to hang out with.

"I've been busy." He made sure to keep it that way. That part of his life was over. He learned his lesson, and he was moving on. It still sent a twist in his gut for his sister Jenny to tell his parents the way she had. It wasn't her place. He and Cade had made an agreement, and he'd say to his parents when he was ready. It would take him a bit not to feel the sting. His sister always had a way of doing that to him, which is why he tried to avoid her most times.

Eventually, he would have to let it go. He would forgive her because he wasn't going to make any more bets or get involved in any more shady deals of trying to help people. His days of horse races and taking questionable jobs to keep his business were long over.

He had debts to finish paying and a future ahead thanks to Cade loaning him what he needed to set things straight with a loan shark and Michael spreading the word through his family to get him better hauling gigs.

Plus, he couldn't imagine not seeing Alison each day.

As the weeks went by, he felt more certain she was God's perfect gift to him.

He prayed he wouldn't screw it up, and she'd be able to accept his past. Otherwise, he wasn't sure how he'd get along with Jenny, and her goodwill barbs and his mother's good intentions pulled at him.

"You still helping out at that horse rescue with your sister?" Rachel asked.

"That's what I do, rescue, and haul horses." Josh headed toward his truck, trying to make a polite escape.

"You might want to take a run down to your old friend Levi's place."

A sour taste formed in his throat. "What's he got down at his place these days?"

Rachel laid her hand on the side of his truck, right below a patch he tried to fix from rusting. "Jake took me down there last week. Don't tell Dad. He doesn't like Jake or Levi or any of them I hang out with. But, it smelled like something died in there, and there was a white horse that looked like it'd had a mud bath and hadn't been let out in months. No one's been cleaning the stalls."

Josh had promised to stay out of trouble. He shook his head. What Levi did at his place and with his animals wasn't his business. He couldn't go getting involved. "You should call the humane society if you're concerned."

"And get in trouble when Levi found out it was me? Then get in trouble with Dad for hanging out there? Geez, Josh. I figured you'd be the one to check it out. You always seem to favor the long shots."

"Call the humane society. I've got to go. It was nice seeing you, Rach."

"Yeah. Whatever."

He got in the truck and drove away. He wasn't far from Levi's house. Only a few miles past the fields of where the stakes races took place at night. Then Josh heard a voice in his head. His hands got sweaty. He shook his head and cleared his thoughts. *No, Lord. I promised. I'm not going back there.*

Lead us not into temptation.

The fan on his heater whined, and Josh gave it a good slap. Besides, he needed to get his heater fixed so he could take Alison on another date without her getting cold.

It warmed up, and by Wednesday, there wasn't a speck of snow left on the ground. Members of the Silver Stirrups Riding Club all showed for the trail ride. On the first Wednesday in the month, the club always had lunch after the ride, so Alison made a big Crock-Pot of chili and corn bread ready for them when they returned.

Dwight came down from the house, and they assembled in the barn's lounge area. Alison had a small heater running to take off the chill as it clung inside the interior of the barn.

Josh unsaddled and gave Destiny a good rub down. He slipped a carrot in her feed bin and gave her praise for a good ride. He could smell the chili and hear Maddy's rosy voice as she told the others a joke that filled the barn with laughter.

Dwight walked with a cane, his shoulders bent. A sling on his arm. "Take a break, boy, get some chili while you can. My granddaughter makes the best chili in the county."

"Be there in a minute." Josh slid Destiny's stall gate closed.

"You do that," Dwight said, unmoving.

Josh turned and saw the man's eyes locked on Destiny. "I can take her back to the rescue with me later. I know this stall belongs to you, sir."

Dwight shook his head. "You keep that horse here. A trail master needs a good horse, and that stall belongs to that horse now. I suppose I'll have to talk to that gal at the rescue about leaving this mare here."

Josh held back his joy in finding Destiny a home at Windy Knoll. "That'd be Sarah. I can hook you up with the paperwork and all that."

"You do that," Dwight said and pointed his cane up the aisle. "There's Randy. It seems he smelled the chili, too, and brought a friend."

Josh glanced over and saw Connor and waved. "Connor Dixon, he's a police officer and friend of my dad."

"Is that right?" Dwight asked.

"I asked him to help find out what happened to Alison's horse."

"So she said." Dwight leaned on his cane. "I leave you to your business. You make a good trail master. My granddaughter did well choosing you."

"Thanks." Josh resisted reaching out to steady the man when he wobbled a little moving forward. Randy gave Josh a cross look, and it made him wonder what he'd done now for the older man to give him with such a hard look.

"Nice day for a ride." Connor offered his hand, and Josh shook it.

"Nicer than most we've had." Josh made sure the stall latch locked. The last thing they needed was Destiny trying to put her nose in the chili.

"I called the clinic, and Jenny said I could find you here. It looks like I got good timing."

"What's up?"

"Mind if we take a walk?" Connor asked.

Josh spotted Alison busy talking in a group with Maddy, Dorothy, and Ed.

Josh turned away and headed outside with Connor. "You found something?"

"I asked to review the file. Not something normally done, but they let me since the detective is dealing with a fresher case."

Because there is a ton of crime going on in the town of Shelbyville, but Josh held his sarcastic tongue. He nodded and listened.

"I went back through the surveillance camera feed for here in the barn. The only ones in this barn were Randy and Alison, but then I saw something interesting, and I wanted to show it to you." Connor pulled out his phone and pulled up a video.

"Josh, I've known you since you were learning to walk. I haven't been able to decide whether you came to me for help to get you out of trouble, or this is some sort of play for you to get the girl and look the hero."

Josh's brows furrowed. He watched the video, knots tying up inside him. It was dark and he was seeing the view from the camera at the outside corner of the barn.

"Are you saying I did this? I don't see anything on this video but shadows and darkness."

"Neither did I until there." Connor paused the video, used his fingers to widen the screen, and blow up the image. "Your trailer still have a tail light out on the back?"

"I fixed it," Josh crossed his arms.

"How long ago?"

"I don't know. A while ago." Josh didn't like where this was going. "Besides, a missing light can't condemn a man."

Connor switched the dark picture and showed the plate on the back of the trailer. "That's yours."

"You can only read the first three letters."

"It's enough of a match to make you a suspect. Listen, your dad told me about the gambling and your brother-in-law paying your debts after getting crossed with the wrong people. A horse like that would bring a few thousand dollars."

"I didn't take Alison's horse. I hadn't set foot at this ranch in years until I came with Michael when Dwight's horse broke its leg."

"Can you prove it?" Connor asked. "Where were you on November twelfth?"

"How am I supposed to know? What night of the week was it?"

"Thursday."

Josh lifted his cap and scratched his head. Paused. Standing outside a few feet away, Josh saw Alison's face pale. Randy clasped a hand on her shoulder and patted it before he turned to walk away.

"Alison?"

"You found something? You found Gus?"

Connor turned toward her. "No. I'm sorry."

"But you found something, right? Randy said you asked him a bunch of questions."

"I did. I wanted to be sure I got as many facts as possible."

"But you asked about Josh. What's going on?"

Connor cleared his throat.

"The camera feed caught a corner of the trailer in the distance that took Gus away."

Alison's eyes widened. "It was dark."

"But Connor's the best. He was able to look over the video and catch what the others didn't," Josh said

"That's why you're here." Hope filled Alison's voice, making Josh cringe inside. He would have to be the one to tell her, and he shifted from one foot to the other.

"I did. Although it might not be what we think it is," Connor said.

"What is it?"

Josh shoved his hands in his pockets. "It looks like it was my trailer that took Gus away."

Alison's eyes got bigger.

Connor put his phone away.

Josh gave her a moment, watching her face go from excited to horrified. "Your trailer?"

Her words stabbed him in the chest. "You took Gus?"

"No. I did not," Josh growled.

"But it was your trailer?" Alison grew paler by the minute. "Jason said you did it, and I didn't believe him. I mean, how could you? Then Randy said he heard you owed money and that you took jobs hauling no matter what or where the money came from. Please tell me it's not true."

Josh felt sick.

Connor placed a hand on Josh. "I need to get going. I will need you to come to the station and answer some questions. You'll need to think where you were on that day. At least where you parked your truck and trailer that can verify it."

Josh swallowed hard and nodded. Where was he on November twelfth? Thursday?

"We'll figure this out," Connor said.

"There's chili in the barn if you want to grab a bowl before you go," Alison said.

"Thank you, but my wife packed my lunch today." Connor left them.

Wheels turned in his head while Alison turned those big sorrow-filled eyes on him. All Josh could hear was Alison saying her ex had tried to accuse him of taking her horse.

Josh headed for his truck.

"Josh?"

He ignored her.

"Where are you going?" she tried to keep up with him, the anger building in her voice, mirroring the anger filling him.

"I've got something I need to do."

"I'm going with you." She rushed to get ahead, the color coming back in her cheeks.

"You'd best stay here. Take care of Destiny for me." He got in his truck, making sure to keep the doors locked.

"What about Gus? What about us?" Alison called.

Without finding Gus, Josh feared there would be no him and Alison. He had to get home, look at his hauling schedule from the past few months, and talk to Cade.

Tears filled Alison's eyes. Josh tried not to think of them. She stomped her foot and yelled at him, but he drove away.

The last thing he ever wanted to do was hurt her. He didn't deserve her, but she deserved the truth. And so did he.

He loved her too much.

It broke him, it bent and snapped and widened in a place he couldn't explain. And he couldn't even tell her.

As Josh drove back home, he tried to remember where he went and what he did or who he hauled for that day. There was no doubt in his mind he hadn't ever picked up a spotted leopard Appaloosa.

Back at the clinic, he found Jenny in her usual spot at the computer and Mrs. Miller sorting through folders behind her.

In the corner, little Dillon sat in a playpen, the young toddler stacking blocks and knocking them over with a plastic truck.

Not bothering with pleasantries, Josh went straight for the file room and pulled a drawer out of the cabinet where his sister kept his hauling records. Never one for paperwork, Jenny handled the bookkeeping for his business and helped him keep his taxes straight.

"What are you looking for?" Slowly, Jenny moved into the room. "We've pulled all the files for today."

"I need to know where I was in November."

"Okay." Jenny crossed her arms and gave him one of her disbelieving looks.

"I mean it, Jen. Connor showed me a video, and it's my trailer that picked up and took Alison's horse away that night."

"Did you?"

"Did I what?" Josh picked through the folders coming to the one labeled "November."

"Haul away the horse and not say anything."

He didn't like the tone she used. Lord help the child she brought into this world. She sounded like their mother when she was on the verge of giving a scolding.

"Seriously?" He couldn't believe she would ask him that. Oh, no. He could. Josh pulled out the folder.

"You know, Jen. I'm tired of you always thinking you know best and are the only one to make things right when things aren't wrong in the first place."

She put her hands over her belly. "I'm sorry I asked." She turned to walk away. "If this is another one of your deals gone wrong, Cade can't get you out of it this time."

Josh slammed the file drawer closed. "I have never stolen anything in my life. Especially a horse."

"I didn't say you did." She held her head high as she walked away.

Josh opened the file, spread it across the top of the file cabinet, and searched through the papers. Thursday, November 12th, he hauled two workhorses to the sale that evening and delivered a standardbred to an Amish farm the next morning.

He slapped the folder closed. Pinching his nose, he leaned against the file cabinet. Besides being at the horse sale that evening, he often kept his trailer parked beside the barn over at the rescue while Michael kept his parked at the clinic.

How many other livestock trailers had the same three letters on their plate as his? Connor would have checked.

Josh walked back out. Jenny sat again, looking up as he came out. "Find what you're looking for?"

"I didn't do it."

"Did you tell Alison that?" Jenny made a point to gather up scattered papers on her desk.

"She won't believe me if I did."

"Then maybe she's not the one for you."

Josh curled his hand into a fist. "Maybe you need to mind your own business."

"Maybe if you'd cool your head for a minute, you'd see I'm trying to help you."

"I don't need your help," he growled.

"Fine." Jenny shrugged. "I won't tell you that your girlfriend called me concerned about you. She doesn't think you stole her horse. It seems to me, you stole her heart."

"Alison called here?"

Jenny sighed.

"What did you tell her?"

"Things I probably shouldn't." Jenny winced. "That I've got a big mouth, and you borrowed money from Cade, and I might have mentioned I think you love her."

Josh flexed the muscle in his jaw. Jenny gave him a half smile and waited while the last bit of what she said sunk in. He could handle the first part. "Are you going to propose for me, too?"

"I'm sorry. Really, I am." And she looked it.

The bell above the door chimed, and Mrs. Miller stepped up to greet the older woman with a fluffy cat in her arms.

Dillon fussed in the playpen. Standing and bouncing while holding on the side, the little guy started to cry, and Josh had never seen his sister look more miserable. He walked over to Dillon and picked up the little guy much quicker than Jenny. One feel of Dillon's damp front and Josh figured he'd fuss too.

"I'll forgive you on two conditions," Josh said.

"Your wish is my command."

"No more talking to other people about my business without my permission first." Josh held up his hand as Jenny's mouth opened. "Good intentions included."

She closed her mouth. Tears brimmed to her eyes. "I don't know what has gotten into me lately."

Josh laughed. His sister would never change, and he prayed motherhood helped change her perspective.

"But okay. And what's the other?" she asked.

He handed her Dillon. "This should about make us even."

Jenny made a face, and Josh tried to hold in his laughter until he got out of the clinic.

Chapter Fifteen

The weekend had passed in torture. Josh came and went in the morning before Alison made it out to the barn. He left her sweet little notes and sometimes a gift. The last thing he'd left for her was cherry gloss. She wondered if he was hinting he didn't like her coconut-flavored gloss as it, too, had been a gift from one of her "grandmas" at Christmas.

Randy had told Gramps he wouldn't be coming to the barn in the mornings. His arthritis had gotten worse in his hands, and he promised to watch his nephew's dog while he went away for a few weeks to report for duty in the reserves for the Army.

With Josh's last note and the cherry gloss on her lips, Alison pulled out her phone as it rang, not bothering to check the caller ID.

"Alison. I've got a new client for you."

Alison groaned inwardly. She heard her boss, Rochelle's, voice. After all these years of working for the Shelby County Family Services, Rochelle hadn't taken Alison's request for fewer clients seriously.

Be steadfast, immovable, always abounding in the work of the Lord, the passage from Corinthians whispered in the back of her mind. She'd thought of this verse so often with Jason calling and texting her again and the strain between her and Josh.

Connor hadn't been able to prove it was Josh's trailer, but no other trailers with those same three first letters on the license plate had appeared in the police's efforts to search for the thief who took Gus.

"Alison, are you listening?"

Alison blinked and realized Rochelle was on the line while her mind had taken a train of thought of its own.

"I can't, Rochelle." Whatever Rochelle had asked, Alison had told her she needed to back down and take care of Gramps and help more with the Silver Stirrups Riding Club. With the weather getting nicer, some of the members would be coming out more often to ride than on the weekly trail ride.

"Alison, you know we're understaffed."

"We're not understaffed. There is more of a need than what we are staffed for, which is different. Hire someone."

"We're looking. In the meantime, I need you to help fill in."

Alison chewed on her lip. She walked down the aisle, past Destiny's stall and pausing near Gus's empty stall. She looked at all the horses and shook her head, the guilt rising seconds ago settling in her gut.

"I've been 'filling in' for years. Listen, Rochelle, I'll keep the clients I have until spring, but I can't take on any more or replace any in my schedule. I need to cut back to part time. I told you Gramps needs me here."

Destiny, at the sound of Alison's voice, turned around and knickered at her.

"I understand, Alison. You've always gone above and beyond when we've needed extra help. A lot of our other support have families and children, and they stick to the children's support in the day."

"I'll pray you find someone to help."

"Can you at least —"

Alison cut her off before she finished, too afraid she'd cave and agree. "No. I can't."

"Then you have the four clients," Rochelle said.

"Three." Alison corrected her.

"Four. Don't forget Fredrickson."

"I thought Fredrickson was a temp fill-in?"

Alison could almost imagine Rochelle's sparkle-painted nails tapping on her desk as she said, "He requested you from now on. He thinks Nadine is too unfriendly."

She could see that about Nadine. The middle-aged woman liked to make a fuss and bustled to get what needed to be done taken care of first and tidy things up. She could see how the well-intentioned woman's manner might reflect as stand-offish to some of their clients.

"Fine. Four. But that's all right now."

"Thank you." Rochelle hung up, leaving Alison standing and staring at the pretty thoroughbred mare that led their trail rides.

"Would you like to go for a walk with me?" Alison grabbed the halter and lead by the door. She stepped inside the stall, and Destiny turned away. "I see how you are." She held her hand out and ran it along the horse's side as she approached the thoroughbred's head. "He's not coming until later." If he came at all. Her heart sank a little.

While they'd spent time together, Josh seemed distant. He didn't try to back her in a dark corner to steal a kiss or linger on the porch after he said good night.

The unspoken strain between them stretched as wide as the empty stall beside her, and she didn't want Gus's loss getting between them. She listened to Gramps and Josh talk of horses and clearing new trails for the riding club. Her grandfather had started having supper at the table instead of his chair as he got better. If she didn't know better, she'd think

Gramps looked forward to those talks more than the times Randy came over.

She managed to get ahold of Destiny's head. "Such a pretty girl." She cooed, sliding on the halter and buckling. As soon as the halter when on, Destiny stood and waited for her to secure the lead.

"This is your home now." A piece of her swayed inside, uncertain if Gramps made the decision from grief or reports from the other members of the club's praise of the horse and its trail master.

She couldn't imagine Gramps riding this leggy mare or any other horse after their loss of Mistress. Ed, from the riding club, had his son engrave a plaque, and they attached it to this stall door in memory of Mistress.

Alison blinked back the moisture. Destiny gave her a little nudge. "It's a beautiful day. We should enjoy it while it lasts." And, before Alison had to take off to tend to a client before lunch and Gramps had a doctor's appointment.

As she led Destiny outside, she inhaled the blossoming scents of the farm. As the cold thawed and the sun beat down to keep the clouds away, Alison marveled at how Windy Knoll started to awake from the gloomy season they'd endured.

She and Destiny fell into a comfortable pace. She walked her around the fence line and behind the house. Sometimes she'd take Gus for a walk. Not to ride him, but to walk like old friends. She'd told him everything from grief and disappointments to delights and anticipated events. She'd shared hard decisions, as she shared with Destiny as they walked. The leggy mare hadn't seemed to mind when Alison wrapped her arms around the horse's neck. "I'm in no way replacing him with you. And I told Josh we'd figure this out. He says he had no part in Gus's disappearance, and I believe him." Although Connor sounded certain the last time she spoke with him that Josh's trailer was involved. Alison laughed. "And here I am telling it to a horse."

After the refreshing stroll, Alison checked on Gramps and went to visit the first client on her schedule. Mrs. Lowmiller's dog always yipped and raced around when she visited. Alison shut the dog in another room while she assisted the elderly woman in getting dressed, and they went for a walk around the downstairs of the house. She didn't want the dog to trip Mrs. Lowmiller, and the elderly woman needed to walk more to keep the circulation going in her legs.

Even for a warm day in March, it was still too cold, according to the ninety-one-year-old woman.

"It's the warmest day we've had since winter," Alison said.

Mrs. Lowmiller would have nothing to do with going out today. "It's gonna rain. I can feel it in these old bones."

She'd take the rain over having another snowstorm roll in any day, but cold was cold. Alison shivered, thinking of the chill it left.

She'd missed her morning coffee, so on her way home to get Gramps lunch, she stopped in at the coffee shop on Main Street. The scent of roasted coffee beans and sweet cream welcomed her.

Inside, modern wood and metal tables spread throughout the little establishment. On the back wall, congregated metal glinted in the yellow lights as people took their lunch breaks and met to feed their midday caffeine addiction.

As she approached the counter, Alison noticed a tall, thin man in stained and ripped blue jeans standing at a bar-height table in the corner talking to Jason. His back was to her, but Alison knew those khaki pants and that checkered blue-shirted body anywhere. She hurried to order her latte, and Sue Ellen gave her a special for Gramps. She'd slipped in two brownies, and Alison figured she'd save the brownies to share with Josh when he came around tonight.

Too distracted to notice her, Jason continued to talk to the man, who didn't look at all happy. Alison started to tap her foot, anxious to grab her order and go.

"Momma says that new trail master keeps them on their toes. Dad was grumbling last week he might have to come out there and join you all."

"Sounds like Dorothy. You tell him to come out anytime we'll have to find him a horse." Alison glanced over her shoulder.

"Oh, I'm sure he'll be out." Sue Ellen got the latte and slid it across the counter toward Alison. She followed Alison's gaze. "That's Levi Holtz. I went to school with him. He was a year older than me, but he didn't take much stock in plain girls, always hung with the rougher crowd. I have seen Josh Anderson with him a time or two. Surprised when I saw him come in and start talking to your ex like they were old friends. Didn't take Jason for one to run with that kind of trouble."

Alison's heart sped as the one called Levi shifted his gaze and gave her a nod. Sue Ellen handed her a little bag with the brownies. "Thanks."

Jason's head turned. His surprise left as quick as it came. A slow smile spread across his face. He said something to Levi, and Alison needed to go.

"Tell your Gramps we're all praying for him."

"Thank you again," Alison said to Sue Ellen. Lengthening her stride, she all but ran from the shop, but not quick enough, as Jason caught up to her.

"Hey, what a surprise!"

Not really, Alison thought. She came here often. Jason knew that too. She avoided the place for months, but they had the best caramel lattes in town, and Sue Ellen's family went to the same church with hers. She liked to support small businesses and people she knew.

"I've got to go, Jason. I'm running late, but it was good to see you." She tried to hurry away. Jason kept up with her.

"Don't you want to know who that guy is back there?"

"It's not my business," she said.

"It should be."

"I'm sorry you think so." Two men having coffee could mean several different things in the world today, but knowing Jason often met with clients outside the office, the man was probably a prospective client. It wasn't her place to make assumptions on first appearances.

"I only met with him to see if he had information about Gus."

That made her stop and stare at Jason. Thankfully, the cap was sealed on her latte, or she would have spilled the hot liquid over her hand. "Why are you doing this?"

"Because Gus is important to you, and I want you to be happy."

"The cops are taking care of it. Leave it to them, or if you know something then you need to tell the police."

"I know Josh Anderson owned the trailer that hauled your horse away. Don't you see, Alison? He's playing you. He took Gus and sold him because he needed money. It's not the first horse he's stolen."

"Josh doesn't steal horses." Alison resumed going to her vehicle.

"No, he *rescues* them." Jason used his fingers to make quotes.

"Tell the police. I need to get going."

She got in her car, Jason scrunching his face and causing creases to fold in his brow. His eyes narrowed on her, and she tried not to let it bother her. She drove away, waiting until she got out of town to let her shoulders relax and sip at the latte, which had started to cool.

What would it take for Jason to understand she wasn't coming back this time? Maybe if she and Josh got married. That was a big one. He hadn't even proposed! She tried to clear her head and her heart from the emotions running into Jason unlocked.

She put down her latte and picked up her phone, then put it back down. She spoke with her mother the day before and got the lowdown on her family happenings in Georgia.

She missed them. Part of her wondered if she should pack up and go to Georgia. There was no way Gramps would be convinced to leave Shelby County. Maybe a vacation? The last vacation she took to the beach with Jason, and Alison had to admit she hated the sticky sand and got bored while Jason played golf or insisted on reading financial articles on the deck of his parents' rented condo.

She couldn't leave. Not Gramps, and not with Gus gone. Especially, her heart skipped a beat as she decided she couldn't leave Josh.

"He didn't do it," she whispered.

Inside the old farmhouse, she found Gramps and Randy laughing and talking over reheated lasagna and coffee.

Gramps's color had come back. She checked her watch to make sure they had time. She didn't want him to be late for his doctor's appointment.

"We saved a piece for you," Randy said.

"It's in that contraception you call a microwave." Gramps pointed in the kitchen.

Alison would say Gramps was feeling much better than several weeks ago. It lightened her heavy mood.

"You bring a pie?" Randy asked.

Alison held up her bag, "Brownies for Josh."

"Nothing for me?" Gramps huffed.

"I'll take you out after your appointment," she said.

Randy rose from his chair and took his plate in the kitchen.

Gramps watched Randy go. "He came here to tell me something you probably will want to hear."

By the tone in Gramps's voice, Alison took her bag into the kitchen and braced herself for the bad news.

Instead, he told her something she had been unprepared to hear.

Chapter Sixteen

It was slow for a Thursday night. Ben stayed in the auction ring, and Josh offered to stay out at the dock for any late drop-offs while Charlie chased things through and kept them in the right pens.

Charlie's whistle got drowned out by the auction until he would get close, resting his arms on the ledge of the check-in window of the small booth under the stairs going up to the floating walkways above the pens.

Alison texted him and sent him kissy faces. He sent her back a grinning emoji while Charlie couldn't see him.

He hadn't heard from her for a few hours and it nearly killed him in that stretch of time not to call her. He missed her all day and hardly saw her the day before. Ever since Connor's visit to the stables and Josh looking for any record of what he did on that day in November, he had been racking his brain to come up with an answer.

He watched for Charlie to go and swap out a set of little Shetland ponies a dealer had dropped out an hour ago to prance through the ring. In Charlie's absence, Josh helped himself to the computer files and the security feeds.

Thank goodness Hank Bailey had invested in new computer equipment and upgraded the security cameras last fall. Josh found the feed for the date in question, hoping to see himself to prove to Connor this is where he was, and his trailer had been parked in the lot outside looking to pick up new business.

Josh fast-forwarded through it, and paused and switched off the screen when Charlie would come past him. One of the dealers from Tennessee brought in a pretty black walking horse.

"She's a stepper," the dealer winked. "Be sure to keep a hold of her."

Josh held onto the mare, noticed the horse's eyes weren't quite right, and held on to her as the dealer finished the paperwork to enter the sale.

"You got a number ready?" Charlie called.

Josh glanced at the paper. "Make her fifty-six."

The dealer fixed his hat and headed back to his truck. As he walked past, the horse took a swipe at him and knocked Josh against the wall. Josh kept hold of the horse. The dealer swore, hit the animal with his hat on the flank, and moved away much faster than he started.

"I take it he got on her wrong side." Charlie chuckled.

"You take her to the pen. I'll grab the chalk pen." Josh grabbed the pen and made sure to keep a safe distance behind. Once in the holding pen, Charlie held onto the horse while Josh stepped up on the boards, reaching over and writing the number on the horse's rump that would wash off later for the new owners.

The Tennessee Walker stood quiet, and Charlie held on until he got out of the pen, and Josh closed the gate while Charlie slipped out. The horse sniffed around, and from the other side of the wall, the auctioneer called for the last bid on the horse in the ring.

Josh paused a minute, accessing the horse. His thoughts went to the Silver Stirrups Riding Club and Dwight's old horse, Mistress.

"She'd be a smooth ride," Charlie called out to him as he headed back to the booth in Josh's absence.

"That she might," Josh said.

The horse ignored him, and if Josh didn't think Alison would mind, he'd buy the horse and bring it home with him. A pretty thing like this with a temper would sell above what he had available, so Josh turned and started back for the booth. He had to stop thinking like Sarah, who had a knack for matching people with horses.

On his way back, he saw Charlie sitting in front of the computer, and he lengthened his strides. He grimaced when he saw the security footage up.

"What's this doing up?" Charlie asked.

"I was watching it." Josh shrugged. Usually, they'd play online videos or solitaire games to pass the time between the beginning of the sale and people loading their purchases.

"You were watching the security tapes? Seriously? You can't be that hard up. Is the internet connection not on tonight?"

Josh leaned against the doorway. "Alison's horse went missing on that day. I wanted to make sure it didn't come through here." And he wanted to make sure he had proof he was here and not parked out at Windy Knoll Farms so no more speculations about him could be made.

The fact that Alison believed him, and had left him those brownies earlier at the barn, reassured him why he'd fallen in love with her more these days than when he dated her in high school.

"Why didn't you say what you were looking for?"

Josh should have known he could trust Charlie without the rest of the staff knowing or making a judgment call on him. He glanced around, hearing the sound of a truck, but it went the other way. With the dock open to the cold air at night, he stepped inside the small space closer to the heater.

"White leopard spot Appy a few months ago."

"Got a time frame?" Charlie asked.

"Yeah. November around the twelfth."

"Second week of November." Charlie scratched the side of his face. "Nope. No horse like that walked through here."

"It was months ago. How can you be certain?"

Charlie clicked off the video and clicked into a new file and opened a new video. "White with brown spots, a leopard Appaloosa, you say?"

"Yeah. That's what I'm looking for."

"It didn't come through here, but a horse with those markings is hard to forget. You don't see them that often, you know what I mean? You're looking at the wrong video. These are the loading dock. You'll want the parking lot."

Josh leaned to the side and allowed Charlie to do his thing. "Parking lot?"

"Dude brought the horse in on the wrong day. Wouldn't even come near the loading dock, said something about dying if he did." Charlie scuffed. "Didn't want to mess up his fancy shoes is more likely."

Josh moved out of the way, and let Charlie have the chair to take over the computer. A few minutes later, he pointed. "There. Is that the horse?"

"Matches the description." A man stepped out of the way as if he was afraid to touch the animal. The camera caught bits and pieces of a second person. "Stop. Can you freeze it and enlarge it to see who that is?"

Charlie shrugged. "Not some IT guy, but sure."

A few curses and taps of the mouse and Charlie managed to enlarge the image.

Josh's fingers curled into a fist inside his coat pockets. He would know that face anywhere, and it sent a hard blow to his gut. What was Levi doing there? He had Gus on a lead rope, and Josh recognized the man in the fancy shoes. Alison's ex-boyfriend, Jason, stayed back from the horse, but it was him. The no-good jerk. He took Alison's horse!

"You know them dudes?"

Josh swallowed down the anger boiling up inside him. "You print me a copy of that screenshot, and I'll need you to email that video to a friend of mine at the police station."

Charlie's brows furrowed together. "Ain't that your truck attached to that trailer?"

"Yep." Josh balled his fist.

"This gonna cause trouble?"

"Yep."

Charlie whistled low under his breath.

"Any idea what happened to the horse after this?"

Charlie moved the video along. Jason got in his vehicle and fled the scene. Standing behind a familiar aluminum stock trailer, Levi handed over the lead of the horse to a man in a Stetson hat and green jacket. "That horse could be in any state by now."

"I don't think so." Josh rubbed his chin. He knew that hat. He knew that green jacket.

"Send that file to this email, Charlie." Josh hurried to scribble the email address on a sale bill.

"I need to go see a man — or make that a woman — about a horse."

On his way, he called Connor and left a message on Connor's phone to meet him and gave the address. His fingers twitched over his phone, wanting to call Alison or at least text her, but he didn't want to disappoint her if things went south from what he suspected.

Instead, he called his father. Not something he did very often, but he told his father what he knew and where he was going. Someone had to know, and his father seemed the less dramatic choice given the situation.

"You be careful," Bill said.

Surprised his father hadn't tried to talk him out of it or give him a lecture about taking the law into his own hands, Josh said, "I will."

And that was it. His father told him to call if he needed him. And for the first time in his twenty-eight years, Josh felt like his father finally accepted him for the man he had become.

Not that any of it would matter. He switched his headlights to low as he headed down the road that would bring him back to Cottonwood Acres.

It was well past nine o'clock in the evening, but the lights were on in the house and a light shone down the walkway of the expensive stables where Rick Demoss housed his best jumpers and racehorses. The one thing Josh admired most about Mr. Demoss was the man had a hand in several different parts of the horse world. He trained racehorses, but when little Rachel came along, he started getting involved in the corsage and jumper circles. He had big dreams of Rachel going to the Olympics and getting her the best trainers one could find in the state of Kentucky. Except Rachel would rather race in endurance rides and get lost in the wilds of Kentucky than sit up astride a horse all prim and proper.

This is why, as Josh knocked on the door, he had a feeling she would help him. He tried to think back to his earlier visit. Had she been hinting? Did she know?

The door opened and Rachel stood in her jeans and an oversized sweater.

"Hey, Rach. I need your help."

She quirked a brow.

"Rachel, honey. Who's at the door?" a woman's voice called from inside.

"It's Josh Anderson. He came to pick me up for our date tonight."

"Date?" Josh crossed his arms.

"Kinda late, ain't it?"

Rachel called back, "He had to work tonight."

"Don't stay out all night like the last time, you hear?"

Rachel rolled her eyes. Josh stood and glared at her.

"Don't wait up."

Rachel slipped out the door and closed it.

"What was that?" Josh asked.

"Daddy won't be back until Saturday. If I have to watch one more sappy movie on that Life channel Momma watches, I'll throw up."

Josh understood. He wondered how Alison could sit and watch westerns with Gramps all the time. Then again, she wasn't there much, and the older gentleman enjoyed them. At least there was action, and you didn't need a box of tissues. Must be a girl thing, but he didn't have time for all that.

"I need to talk to you."

Rachel tapped her foot. "Can we do it in the truck? You know, where it's warmer?"

That wasn't what Josh had in mind. "How about the stables?"

"Fine." Rachel shrugged, "But I figured we'd talk on the way to Levi's."

"The horse is at Levi's?" Josh ran his hand over his mouth. It made sense now. The man in the green jacket and hat was Rick Demoss, but Levi had used Josh's trailer. He assumed the horse would be at Rick's place.

"I told you about the horse at Levi's. Aren't you going to rescue it?" Rachel planted her hands on her hips.

"I told you to call the humane society."

"And get Levi in trouble?" She snorted. "How stupid do you think I am?"

"That's why you told me." Josh would smack himself for his stupidity later. Right now, he would be grateful to find the horse.

"You know, Levi said you were a pushover." She started walking. He could blame her. It might not be winter cold, but the air still carried a bite standing out on the porch.

"You don't have the horse here?" Josh followed her to where his truck was parked.

"Daddy wouldn't let me bring it here. He told Levi he didn't want any part of you and Levi's schemes."

There was more to this than he figured. Rachel continued to talk as he unlocked the truck, and she got in.

He almost hesitated for a moment, considering he hadn't had any other female in his truck since he started seeing Alison. It made him a bit uncomfortable as he shut the door and walked around the other side.

"Please tell me the heater works." Rachel leaned forward to play with the heat control knob.

"Who told you my heater doesn't work?" Josh put on his seat belt and turned on his truck.

"Levi." Rachel rubbed her hands together. Josh reached behind her and pulled the blanket down from over the back that he'd put there for the next time the heater broke and Alison got cold.

"You should at least warn people that the heat doesn't work before you lend them your truck."

As Josh turned his truck around, with the trailer still hitched on the back, and headed toward Levi's place, he clamped his jaw shut. He could feel the muscle twitch in his cheek.

This is what he got for returning a favor to a friend. Not that he and Levi hung out anymore or that he considered Levi a friend since Josh stopped going to the field races and held his promise to Cade and God that he wouldn't bet or gamble anymore.

Even in trying to do the right thing, something terrible had happened. Or had it? Josh wouldn't have had a second chance with Alison or been able to take the role of trail master with the Silver Stirrups Riding Club if Dwight's horse, Mistress, hadn't fallen and rolled on him while out riding.

"Rachel." Josh kept his tone conversational and light. "The horse Levi's got out there at his place. It's a white gelding with brown spots, isn't it?"

"Of course it is." She turned to look at him and clucked her tongue. "He tried to pass it off to Daddy for a lead pony, but Daddy wouldn't have anything to do with whatever deal you and Levi cooked up."

"Me?" Josh tried to keep a cool head, and his hands relaxed as he remembered the way to Levi's. "I didn't have anything to do with this."

"He was using your truck and trailer."

"Your father was with him."

"Really?" She had to think about that for several minutes. "I don't know anything about that."

They rode in silence the rest of the way. Josh felt his phone vibrate in his pocket, but he couldn't answer it.

No one was at Levi's place. No lights on in the old trailer Levi lived in, and only a pole light to illuminate the leaning shack that Levi called a barn. Metal and old pellet boards nailed in every direction held the building together. Josh parked close to the barn, keeping the headlights of his truck on.

Levi's truck was missing, and Rachel got out and walked to the front of the barn.

"Wait."

Rachel glanced over her shoulder. "Why?"

"We can't go in there without permission."

"Since when are you afraid of breaking and entering?"

Josh reached in his pocket and pulled out his phone. He'd missed a call from Cade. No doubt, his father called his brother-in-law. Josh sent a text to Connor with Levi's address. He also texted Cade before he turned on the flashlight feature in his phone.

It wouldn't hurt to make sure the horse was all right.

"You coming?" Rachel had pulled out her phone and used the soft glow from her screen.

"Be careful, and don't touch anything."

Rachel snorted. "It's a barn."

She flung open the door, and the stench hit Josh, twisting his stomach, and he almost retched. He covered his mouth and nose. Inside to his left, an eye gleamed in the darkness against the light of his phone.

Josh stepped over a pitchfork laying prongs up, and Rachel kicked aside a small bucket. As they approached, the horse shied back, and Rachel spoke to it as not to have it spook. "It's okay, buddy. We're here to get you out of this muck."

What Josh saw caused his insides to roll. Standing in months of its own waste, the horse could have been any color from white to black. In the dark and by the light of their phones, the horse shied back into the corner of the stall.

"One of us is going to have to go in there and get it out."

"Not yet." Josh stepped over, careful not to step on anything or upset the horse. "He's going to freak, so stay back."

And the horse jumped as Josh predicted as he took several pictures, letting his flash on his phones illuminate the stall.

The horse slammed back against the wall, shaking the structure. Rachel stepped behind Josh. "Are you trying to kill us or just the horse?"

"Let's step out of here for a minute and get some fresh air. I'll pull the truck up, and we'll get him out of here."

"About time!" Rachel strutted out of the barn.

"Careful of the pitchfork," Josh said.

Rachel spotted it in the dark and reached down to pick it up when the sound of a vehicle pulling in caught their attention.

"Who is that? Is that Levi?" Rachel froze.

"Call the police. Tell them where we are and what we found." Josh walked out ahead of her as he heard a door slam.

"You crazy? We'll get in trouble for trespassing."

"And we'll be in bigger trouble for horse theft if you don't."

"Not me," Rachel said. "You."

"Then call and report me. Just call the police!" Josh made it several steps out of the barn when Levi stepped around Josh's truck between the headlight beams.

Chapter Seventeen

"What you doing out here, Josh?" Levi asked. He leaned a bit and nodded. Josh glanced behind him to where Rachel had stumbled outside of the shack. "Rach, baby. What's this?"

"You tell me." Josh slid his finger over his phone and pressed the record button for his phone's video function to start.

"You trying to steal my girl?" Levi moved closer, smelling of alcohol and smoke from one of the local bars.

"She's all yours." Josh held his ground, his hand squeezing around the phone as his heart sped. He had known Levi for a few years, and standing here with Levi under the alcohol's influence would only cause more trouble. He didn't want to fight.

"I thought you said Josh knew about the horse." Rachel swayed her hips as the shadows danced around her, and she stepped into the beams of light. "I told you before I didn't like how you were treating that horse."

"And I told you, woman, to mind your own business!" Levi huffed.

"I'll be taking the horse," Josh said.

"Sorry, man. You can't rescue this one." Levi widened his stance and lifted his chin.

Josh glanced over at Rachel. "Open the back of the trailer, would you? There's a lead in the side door if you need one."

Levi growled. "I'm making good money off that horse. You're not taking it anywhere."

"It won't do anyone any good if it's dead." Josh tried to stay calm. Levi walked up, got in his face.

"That old man send you here? Well, you can tell him the deal is off." Levi's breath made Josh turn his face away. "And don't you think you can come here and get in on it. Rachel. You open that gate, sweetheart, and you'll be facing a whole lot of hurt."

"You open that gate, Rachel. He ain't gonna touch you." Josh's voice deepened as he allowed the anger to slip through that boiled inside him since Levi arrived.

When Levi tried to step around him, Josh stepped in his way. "How much did he pay you?"

Levi tilted his head, taken aback by Josh's question, then laughed. "Why? Are you gonna try and buy that horse from me? Well, you can't. It ain't for sale."

"You tried to sell it to Rick."

"Rent it, not sell. Man, that old nag in there is my monthly security check. It ain't for sale. I tried to warn that idiot not to involve the old man, too many people. You understand. It's why you're here. Sorry rescue boy, but this cut is all mine." Levi shoved Josh back and started around to the trailer as Rachel the gate swung open.

"Rachel, don't you go in that barn."

"Rachel, go get the horse."

Levi turned and swung. He caught Josh under the jaw with his fist and sent Josh sprawling on the ground. Josh's phone flew from his hand.

Rachel raced to the barn, and Levi went after her. Josh leaped at Levi, grabbing him around the legs and pushing him down. They rolled, and Levi kicked Josh in the gut.

Instinctively, Josh's arms went around his stomach. He rolled away, but Levi grabbed him, sat atop him, and Josh raised his arms to block Levi's punches.

"Levi, stop!" Rachel cried.

Josh took advantage of the moment to toss Levi off. They went rolling across the cold dirt and grass. Josh managed to get free and get on his feet. Levi rose, and the two circled each other.

"I don't want to fight you." Josh placed a protective hand over his ribs, sure one was badly bruised.

"You get in that truck and forget you ever came here. Understand? And if you're smart, you'll stay away from Ward's woman. He's got plans, and he won't finish paying me if you mess them up."

Another set of lights lit up the drive as another vehicle pulled behind Levi's truck.

"Josh!" Alison's voice rang out. Behind her, two more cars pulled along the side of the road, and men came running to the shack.

"Alison?" Josh looked in the direction of her voice. Levi swore and came at Josh a second time. He slammed Josh up against the front of his truck.

"Police. Freeze!"

Levi growled, shoved Josh again, and took off for his truck.

He took off across the yard and through the field. A moment later, another vehicle took off in chase.

Alison came around the truck and wrapped her arms around him before he had a chance to peel his back from the truck grill. "Thank you, God. You're okay."

He grunted, not wanting her to let him go, but her tight hold made his ribs hurt as if Levi kicked him again. "What are you doing here?"

Alison pulled back. Connor and another man stepped into the light of his headlights. "You okay?"

"Yeah. I'll live. Rachel is inside, trying to get the horse out." The man beside Connor headed to the shack.

Alison tried to leave him, but Josh held onto her. He needed to feel her safe in his arms for an extra minute. He needed to prepare her just in case. "I don't know if it's Gus."

"It is." Alison kissed him on the cheek. "Randy told me everything."

"Randy?"

"I'll help Rachel. He'll feel better with me." Alison stifled a sob. "I can't believe he's been here all this time." She took off despite Josh's attempt to hold on to her. Josh limped away from the truck.

Randy? Slowly, as the adrenaline dissipated from his system, the sense of what had happened filled him.

"You sure you're fine? I'll call in for an ambulance."

"No." Josh held up his hand, then leaned back against the truck. He needed an extra minute. Levi had shoved him hard. He didn't want to appear weak in front of Alison, even in the dark.

"If we can find my phone, it's probably still video recording."

Connor glanced around and walked over to pick up Josh's phone. It still had power, and the light on the screen made it easier to locate. "This one."

"Yeah. You'll get half a confession on there."

"You should have waited for me."

"You didn't call back." Josh winced.

"We have what we need. We have what we need from Randy's confession. There are officers out picking up Jason Ward as we speak. It seems he thought, if the horse went missing and he found it, the girl would come back to him."

"Stupid," Josh hissed.

"That's where I was when I got your call. Let's get you checked out." Sirens sounded in the distance.

Josh shook his head. "I need to go help Alison."

"I think they can take it from here," Connor said.

Once the EMTs decided Josh didn't have any serious injuries other than a few painful bruises, they let him go on his way. Connor gave them permission to take the horse to the clinic. Alison followed him in her car.

An officer gave Rachel a ride home after they got done questioning her. The call came in that Levi had been arrested after running his truck into a fence post, trying to escape.

Michael met Josh out at the clinic stables. Under the bright lights, the horse looked worse, with rub marks on the side of its face from the halter, matted hair, and having been denied one too many meals. It wouldn't surprise him if Levi had only given the horse hay, and the animal had trampled it into the muck of the dirty stall rather than eating most of it.

Levi wouldn't have risked letting the horse out in the corral for someone to spot it.

Alison stood petting the animal's face, tears streaming down her face.

Josh rubbed her back. "It's okay, Ali. We got him back."

"Is he okay?" Alison asked.

"Nothing a good grooming and some groceries won't fix, but we'll keep him here a few days. I'll check him over more thoroughly in the morning."

Alison rested her cheek against the horse's face. Gus jerked away. Josh pulled Alison back. "He hasn't been handled in months. He'll need some time."

Alison swallowed hard. Josh could see her pushing back the disappointment of Gus's reaction.

"Come on. It's been a long night. I'll take you home. Gramps must be worried."

Josh kept his arm around her, steering her away.

"I'm sorry we woke you," she whispered to Michael.

"I was awake. I was up with Dillon." Michael covered the next yawn with his hand. "Good night."

Josh unhooked his trailer and left it parked by Michael's trailer near the clinic's barn before going back to get Alison.

"I can't believe he's here."

Josh wrapped an arm around her. "He's safe, and we'll have him back at home in his own stall in no time."

"I got so scared." Alison turned in his arms. "When Randy told me what Jason did, and he helped him, I — I couldn't believe it."

Josh kissed her on the forehead after she settled in his truck.

"He confessed."

"Jason made him believe he was doing a good thing that he was helping get us together again. Then you came along, and he refused to give Gus back when Randy insisted it had been long enough."

"It's over now. Gus is back."

She looked at him in the dim light of the interior of his truck. Her pale face and big eyes tugged at him in all the right places. He wanted to blurt what he felt and held back, knowing he could wait a little longer.

"Who was the girl in the barn?"

"Rachel Demoss. Her father owns Cottonwood Acres. Jason tried to get Rick to take Gus on as a lead pony in his stables."

"Serious?"

"Cross my heart. I wouldn't lie to you."

"I should have listened to Jason. None of this would have happened. I'm sorry you got pulled in this."

Josh reached over and took her hand as he drove. "You couldn't have known."

She fell silent, the adrenaline rush of tonight fading from them both. Josh held onto her hand, his thumb rubbing back and forth across her wrist. His fingers entwined with hers. Fear tightened his hold as he felt he couldn't let go of her.

He got it, the shock still fresh in her system. Her hand felt colder than usual. His heart pumped more wildly than all those times he spied her at school, and he chose to step away. Only he wasn't stepping away anymore. The L-word was at the tip of his tongue and he knew he had to tell her.

He waited until they got to the house. He had no choice but to let go of her hand to get out of the truck.

On the porch, he took her in his arms. He kissed her, pouring his heart and soul, and every tender-hearted thought he had for her into that kiss.

"I'm sorry this happened," Josh said.

"Me too," she whispered. "I never thought Jason would go to such extremes to kidnap Gus."

"Some men will do anything to hold on to the one they love. It's not your fault." He touched her cheek, brushed away the last residue of her tears. "Alison, this might not be the best time, but timing isn't something that has always been in our favor, so I'm just going to say it. I love you. I've known you long enough to know you think this has something to do with something you did wrong. Stop.

"There's no way you could have known this would happen. You're the most caring and compassionate person I've ever met. You think of others always before yourself. And it's one of the many reasons I love you."

And there he said it. Twice.

Alison's eyes grew large. She pulled away from him. "You love me?"

"That's what I said." His entire world seemed to suspend on her reaction. She frowned, and it caused the elation to come crashing down.

"No."

"No?" Maybe she hadn't heard him right. "Ali, I said I love you. I've loved you from the first time I saw you in high school, and I should have told you then. So, if anyone is at fault, it's me. I tried to do the right thing by my sister and Sarah, but I didn't think —"

Alison put her hand over his mouth. "I love you, too."

Relief started to flood his system. He pulled her closer, but Alison dropped her hand from his mouth and stepped back.

"What's wrong?" Her words didn't match her actions. He wanted to kiss her, hold her, and not ever let her go.

"I can't."

"You said you love me. I love you. It's not like I asked you to marry me." Josh growled, angry with himself. This wasn't the reaction he figured she would give him. They were tired. Maybe he should have waited. Too much had happened tonight. Perhaps this was too soon.

Good going, Anderson, you always were one to jump in without using your head.

"Jason did," Alison whispered. "Several times. I told him no. It didn't feel right. Not like us. But then seeing what Jason did to get me back, I can't. I'm sorry, Josh."

"You're thinking of going back to him? Alison, the guy's going to jail. He *stole* your horse to try and manipulate you." Josh's voice rose with his panic.

"No. That's not what I'm saying." Her hands waved. Her voice strained. He braced for female hysterics on the verge of his own walls going up at her rejections.

"I'm trying." He ran his hands over his face. She appeared on the verge of tears.

"Listen, we're both tired. We'll talk more about this tomorrow."

"Tomorrow won't change what has happened."

"No, it won't. But tomorrow we're going to go clean up Gus and get him ready to come home. Tomorrow we're going to move forward, and we're going to do it together."

"Why are you being like this?" She sniffled.

Josh tilted her head. He wouldn't say it a third time. Instead, he put his finger on her lips, leaned in, and kissed her forehead. Lowered to kiss the tip of her nose, and dipped to press her lips to his in the sweetest kiss he ever imagined.

"Get some rest. I'll see you in the morning."

Josh walked to his truck. He waited until Alison went inside before resting his forehead on his hands. Gripping the steering wheel, he took a moment to pray and ask God to surround Alison in His love.

Chapter Eighteen

Josh rose before the sun and started his duties early. He brought Gus some carrot pieces and apple slices to munch on as Josh worked at getting the large clumps of dried mud and manure from the horse's coat.

"I thought they said he was white," Cade waltzed in the clinic right on time as usual. Josh had the coffee brewing in the clinic stables. Cade brought fresh blueberry muffins baked that morning by Jenny.

"You spend the night here?"

"What makes you think that?" Josh worked the curry brush down Gus's flank. Either Gus didn't care or the horse wasn't feeling his oats to protest.

"Maybe 'cause it looks like you slept in those clothes, and you skipped shaving this morning. Or hey, maybe you're going for the rugged look, but Jenny will give you a hard time if she sees you. Giving you a warning."

Josh tossed the brush in the bucket and stepped out of the stall.

"I'll worry about me as soon as this guy is cleaned up. I'm sure Alison will be more interested in him than me when she comes."

"Ouch." Cade walked with a limp from an old rodeo accident. He grabbed a lead and made his way to a horse a few stalls down from Josh. "Heard what happened last night."

Josh decided it best not to discuss last night. One night of prayer couldn't ease the troubles of the heart, but it was a good start. He prayed for Alison, for the hurt and the past grief that must have surfaced with finding Gus. He prayed for her comfort and peace no matter what his role became in his life. He learned some time ago he couldn't tell God what he would do and always expect it to work out.

"I'm gonna use the wash stall. It's a bit chilly, but Gus here will be white when Alison gets here. Connor will be by soon to confirm this is the right horse."

"You'll need to go with Michael this morning. The nicer weather and I've got two therapy horses here in the clinic. I can't spare the extra time."

Josh wiped his dirty hands on his pant legs. He planned on staying here and helping Sarah over at the clinic to keep close when Alison arrived.

"That'll work for today, but I have to haul tomorrow morning."

"Tell Jenny. She'll have to adjust the schedule."

"I thought she was taking a break before the baby is born."

Cade opened the stall door, glanced back, and gave Josh a look. Josh chuckled. "Right. Will do."

Josh led Gus to the fancy wash stall Michael had designed into the clinic stables when he'd built this structure a few years ago. The temperature-controlled stall would keep Gus from catching a cold, and the special shampoo made the gelding smell more like a disinfected old saddle than a dozen roses.

It took Josh most of the morning and several scrubbings, but when he finished, a white horse with brown spots walked out of the washing station.

Josh crosstied Gus and wiped the excess water from him. He cleaned his hooves and noticed Gus was missing a shoe.

He heard movement down the aisle and figured Cade had returned with one of the therapy horses he had taken for a walk to build its strength back in whichever leg it had injured. It wasn't Josh's job here to know which horse hurt what. He kept them clean, bedded, and fed when he wasn't running somewhere to haul or help Michael on a call or Sarah at the rescue.

"Tell Jenny to call Hank. Gus is missing a shoe, and the back left is coming loose."

"He's coming out to our place on Friday, so I'll add Gus to his list of horses." Alison's soft voice sent goose bumps up his arms.

He let Gus's foot down and straightened. She looked lovely in a pair of leggings and knee-high boots. She had on a long sweater with a belt at the waist. He wondered if she had come from visiting a client or was on her way out to see one.

She'd twisted her hair up, leaving a few strands hanging by her cheek.

"You look pretty this morning."

A little shade of pink spread across her cheeks. Josh patted his chest, his clothes wet and damp in places with mud and manure smeared on his arm.

"It looks like you've been busy."

"Gus and I wanted to look our best for when you got here. Only you surprised me. I wasn't expecting you this soon."

"I have a client this morning, Mrs. Woods, and then I need to check in with Rochelle for some paperwork. I wanted to stop in and see Gus. I was almost afraid yesterday was a blur, kind of like a dream, and I wanted to make sure he was here." Alison walked up to Gus's head and kissed him square between the eyes. This time, the horse didn't shy.

"I'd hug you, but you're all wet," she told the horse. "I missed you so much."

Josh's chest tightened. She talked to the horse. He gave her space. He cleaned up his grooming tools and headed for another cup of coffee. He would have to head out with Michael in less than an hour, and he needed to change.

He wanted to say something to her. He put his foot in his mouth last night and decided best leave it at that.

"I need to change and head out on a call with Michael. Can you put him back in the stall to your right when you're done visiting?"

Alison glanced over at him, her expression blank. "Of course."

Josh decided he'd better leave. "I'll see you later."

"Will you bring Gus?"

"Talk to Michael. He says it's okay. I will."

When Alison's phone rang later in the day, she hadn't expected it to be her mother. "Is something wrong?"

"Gramps called me," her mother said. "He told me what happened. I'm so happy you got Gus back."

Alison blinked back the tears prickling in her eyes. Happy tears at hearing her mother's voice and having her beloved horse back. Her mom had been on her mind most of the day, along with Josh, and everything that had happened. She wanted to talk to her mom and hear her voice.

"Did Gramps tell you it was Jason behind it? He had Randy help him. He hired someone." Alison walked down the sidewalk to get some fresh air while Mrs. Englehart received her dialysis. Alison took her twice a week on rotation, and soon Maryann from her agency would take this task back from Alison on her return from maternity leave.

"It did surprise me, but Jason always was the calculating sort. He didn't try to force you to marry him this time, did he?"

"No." Alison paused to watch an older couple in the hospital parking lot. The man opened the door for the woman, and she smiled at him. "He would have. I know him enough to know he was working his way up to it."

Her mother listened, patiently, as Alison went on about Josh, what happened the night before, and how Josh had scuffled with the kidnapper and Jason's warnings.

"Jason's in jail. I'm sure his parents will have him bailed out before long, Alison. It sounds like Josh cares much more about you than Jason ever could. I never liked Jason or his influence on your life."

"Mom?"

"I have to say it, and you need to listen."

Alison stopped walking.

"You are a strong, intelligent woman. Don't ever let Jason make you think you are not. It sounds like Josh has been honest with you all this time. I think you need to be honest with him."

"I told him I love him."

"You're scared. I hear it in your voice."

"I'm not afraid of Josh." Alison glanced around to make sure no one was listening to her conversation.

"I didn't say you were."

"You said I was afraid."

"You love him. It scares you. After what you went through with Jason, no one could blame you. I called to tell you that I'm coming home."

"What? Why?"

"Your father and I have discussed this. It's only for a little while to help with Gramps and the farm. Scott will be coming for the summer. We want to do this. I know you're not going to pack up and come to Georgia any more than Dad is going to give up the farm. I feel like I need to be there for you and Gramps right now."

"Thanks, Mom."

"I've got a flight scheduled for Thursday. I'll email you the details. Oh, and Alison, talk to Josh. Don't let your past with Jason hold you back if you care about him the way you say you do."

"I won't. I promise."

"I can't wait to see you! And Gus!"

Alison giggled. "And Gramps. You did tell him you were coming, right?"

"He told me not to come," Mom retorted. "You'd think he'd know by now not to try to convince me otherwise."

Alison and her mother said their goodbyes. Her spirit lifted, thinking she would soon see her mother, and Scott was coming this summer.

Earlier that morning, she confirmed with Connor that the horse they recovered last evening was indeed her beloved Gus. She agreed to press charges against the man who stole him and Jason. Even though Randy had cooperated in assisting with Gus's recovery, Alison knew the relationship he would have with her grandfather would never be the same again. In fact, Gramps had told Randy he couldn't come to the stables anymore.

Time would have to work its way into both their hearts. While forgiveness had been granted, Randy broke their trust, and it wasn't something that could be restored automatically.

Alison understood those feelings. They were among the few emotions she could identify. Randy had a kind heart, and she truly believed he had good intentions to try and help Jason and her get back together. She figured he'd heard her sobs and her confessions to Gus in the barn on times she wasn't aware of him in the barn.

Randy had been helping her grandfather with the stables for years. It pained her to have their friendship damaged in this way, and she prayed for the healing of their hearts. Mom coming home would help.

Her mother always had a way of making things better. She tried to warn Alison about Jason's behavior, and in her heart, Alison tried. Taking Gus was extreme, even for her ex-boyfriend. Only she'd known, and without Josh she would have never gotten her beloved horse back.

Josh, the man she loved. The man she pushed away. Fear draped over her like a wet blanket.

It took her months of courage and support to hold firm against Jason's attempts to reel her back into his arms. Then Gus disappeared.

Alison headed back to the hospital. Mrs. Englehart would finish soon and be worried if she came out of treatment and Alison wasn't there. She remembered the bear and the blanket, the ones that Mrs. Englehart brought with her to dialysis. Alison got her a tote and carried it to make it easier for these visits.

"My grandson Bryce got this for me for Christmas," Mrs. Englehart told her every time as she drove her home. She sat with her, anxious to find Josh. She fidgeted and cleaned while Mrs. Englehart went on about her nine grandchildren and three great-grandchildren. Any other time Alison would love to hear about them. She waited patiently for Mrs. Englehart to exhaust herself and nap.

Alison tucked her in and texted Josh while she waited for a family member to come and sit the afternoon with her client.

I need to talk to you.

She stared at her phone and waited. And waited. And cleaned up a pile of sudoku books and crossword puzzles.

Once Mrs. Englehart's granddaughter came after school, Alison went on her way to check Mr. Fredrickson and get back to the clinic to check on Gus. She hoped Josh would be there.

She knew what she needed to do.

And she prayed God would open Josh's heart to understand and accept her decision.

Chapter Nineteen

The clinic was closed by the time Alison got there. A sign on the door gave information to call for emergencies. Alison went to the clinic stables and found them locked. She had at least hoped to check on Gus while she was there.

Stopping over at the rescue stables, she found the place empty of humans. Sarah wasn't home, and Alison got an unsettling feeling. Josh's truck wasn't at the carriage house, and he still hadn't responded to her text.

It was out of her way, but Alison struggled with wanting to go to Cade and Jenny's place. She seemed to remember they lived out at the old Zimmerman place in the opposite direction of home.

But home won out. Without Randy and with Gramps not healed, she had her work cut out for her. Gramps suggested she ask the members of the riding club to help and she didn't want to do that. Although Maddy Pierce had been hanging around taking care of Texas and offered to do what she could before anyone could have guessed Randy would have been involved in Gus's disappearance.

In time she hoped they could all move past this. It wouldn't be something that could be easily forgiven, let alone forgotten. She prayed

could all move forward and was thankful to find Maddy in the barn
en she arrived.

A note on the feed room said she needed to order feed. She
recognized Josh's handwriting, messy and in a hurry, just like him.

"You must be thrilled to have Gus back! Will you be leading the trail
ride on Wednesday?" Maddy approached her, work gloves on her hands,
and her silver strands pushed back behind her ears.

"More than you'll know, but until they release him from the clinic, I
don't think he'll be up to going out on the trail for a few weeks."

Maddy frowned. "That's not Gus in his stall?"

Alison's heart quickened. "Gus is here?"

She hurried down the aisle to Gus's stall. She slid open the stall door,
and Gus came straight to her. He was halterless, but a brand new one
with a lead hung by the door. She ran her hand over the spots on his face
where the old one had rubbed.

Tears prickled her eyes again, touching him, having him back where
he belonged. Her mind went straight to Josh.

"He's a special guy, isn't he?" Maddy stood in front of Destiny's
stall. The mare put her ears back, not impressed by her new next-door
neighbor.

"Yeah. He's always been that steady, reliable thing in my life."

"The horse or the man?" Maddy quirked her brow. "He tried to stick
around, but when he got that call, he had to go. I told him not to worry.
I'll stay and help you feed the horses."

"He had to go?"

Maddy smiled, "He took Jenny to the hospital. Cade was going to
meet them there."

Alison giggled. "That explains why no one was at the clinic or the
rescue."

"Well, I do believe babies take time. It could be a long time at the hospital." Maddy clucked.

"Do you think they'd stay all night?"

Maddy shrugged. "You go on. Ed is coming over and can help do the feeding. Dwight will make sure we get it right and secure the barn. All the horses will be safe, especially Gus."

"I should stay here. I'm not family. I'll see Josh in a few days."

"But you're dating," Maddy said, "You should go. He'd want to see you. Besides, I have a feeling he'd be happy for the distraction."

"I don't know." She wanted to talk to Josh.

"Gus isn't going anywhere. He'll be here. You can check on him when you get back if it makes you feel better."

Maddy's eyes were kind, and her words gave Alison the little push she needed. She checked on Gramps, and he confirmed he could handle taking care of the security and advising Maddy and Ed on doing the feeding.

As she drove out the driveway, Josh's truck pulled in, blocking her from going any further. He parked his truck, got out, and Alison did the same.

"Hey there," she waved at him, wondering if she should have backed up and parked at the barn to let him come in.

Josh leaned against the front of his truck. "I heard you wanted to talk to me." He pulled his phone out of his pocket and flashed it before putting it away.

"You got my text."

"Yeah. I came back as soon as I could."

Alison walked around the front of her vehicle. "How's Jenny?"

"False alarm."

"How terrible that must be."

Josh pushed away from the front of the truck. "She's got another week." He shrugged, his gaze locking on hers. "You said you wanted to talk."

"I did." She giggled. It slipped out. There was nothing she funny about what she planned to say to him.

Josh's eyes never left hers. Her face lit with heat, and she licked her lips, feeling them suddenly go dry. "You didn't text back."

"It's been a busy day." He took another step closer. His gaze alone made her knees go a little weak.

"You brought Gus home."

Josh reached over and brushed her hair back behind her ear. "I said I would, but I don't think that's what you want to talk about."

"No. There is something else I want to tell you."

Josh grabbed her by the upper arms. Not hard enough to hurt her, but firm enough to knot her stomach. "You're not breaking up with me. I told you last night. I love you. I'm not going anywhere."

"Good." She pushed her rising nerves down and slid her arms around him. "I'm not letting you go. Even after you hear what I have to say. I'm not letting you leave me ever again."

"You're not pushing me away?"

She shook her head.

"After last night, I admit I didn't want to answer your text. I don't want to lose you, Alison."

"There are some things I need to tell you. Things I need you to understand."

"It has to do with Jason."

She nodded.

Josh touched his forehead to hers. "Ali, I don't care about your past, but if it makes you feel better to talk about it. Then I'm here to listen."

Gently, his lips brushed hers, and a car turned down the lane. Alison started to lean in for more when Josh pulled back. "I suppose they'll want in to get to the barn."

Alison glanced around him. Her hands curled into this flannel shirt. "That would be Ed. He's coming to help Maddy in the barn since I was headed to the hospital to see you."

She chewed on her lip.

"Then I caught you in time. Why don't we move out of the way? I'll park by the barn, and we can take a walk."

"I'd like that. She glanced back at him, and he winked.

They moved their vehicles out of the way and waved at Ed.

"Why don't we check the fence row?" Josh took her hand, and they fell into step together.

They walked for a bit in silence, the house and barn getting further away, and the sun lowering and the sky darkening. They came to a place where the pasture split and a gate opened to another section of the field with the woods to their right.

"I love this time of day." She wished she could enjoy it more often and hoped with her new work schedule to make it possible. She saw the sun dipping down behind the landscape.

Josh slipped his arm around her. "I know a good place to watch the sunset. Maybe some evening, you'll let me take you there."

"As long as our schedules meet."

"We'll make it work." His voice deepened, and Alison sighed. There was no easy way to tell him about her life before him.

"Jason's allergic to almost everything. Hay, pine, horses, actually most animals. His idea of spending time together is sports and his friends. When I met him, he seemed interested in all the same things, but then I realized it was only a mask. Jason likes things a certain way. He has a plan, and you can't go off plan."

She paused, but Josh didn't say anything. She continued. "He has this way of always doing enough. He'd make me feel guilty, especially when I wouldn't agree to marry him. When no one else was around, he started to slip more and more. Little by little, he admitted we had nothing in common. He went to church because it is what is expected, not because we share the same importance of faith or even family values. I want kids, and he said maybe in a few years one child, but they're expensive, and everything with Jason always comes down to the bottom line numbers."

She let it pour out, the times when Jason made her feel less than enough in front of his friends and how he insisted she work more hours to build her retirement early.

Josh's jaw twitched. His hand curled more around her waist, drawing her in.

"I think Jason hired a detective to check you out. Taking Gus was one of his ploys to get me back, to make sure nothing got in the way of his life plan. He blamed you for taking Gus."

"You had faith in me. I appreciate that."

"Of course I do. I knew you couldn't have done it. It's one of the reasons I love you so much." Alison turned, putting the sunrise at her back. "I suspected a long time ago Jason had something to do with it. I couldn't prove it, and neither Gramps or I could have guessed Randy would have been involved."

"Ali, you had every right to suspect me. It was my truck and trailer. I guess I have some things I need to tell you, too. Then maybe you won't think so highly of me."

"It has to do with your family. Josh, I hope you're not telling me this because I told you about Jason."

"I'm telling you because I respect you, and I want a future with you. I've done some stupid things and got caught up in some bad decisions The other night at Levi's place should have tipped you off."

"Because Levi used your truck and trailer."

"I owed him a favor. He asked to borrow my truck and trailer. I haven't always made the best choices, as I said, and when I found myself in trouble my brother-in-law Cade pulled me out. I owe him. He lent me money, and part of my debt is going to church on Sundays unless I'm too ill or dead."

"Oh, my." Alison pressed her hand to her heart. She never wanted to pry on his business. A new appreciation for his honesty bloomed inside her.

"My choice in careers might not impress my family, but it's my business. It's not much, but I like what I do."

"You don't have to justify yourself to me. I love you for who you are. I've seen you with the members of the club and the way you help at the rescue and the clinic."

Josh took off his hat. Folding the bill in his hands, he said, "I don't have much to offer, Ali. I'm never going to be a nine-to-five kind of guy, but neither am I going to tell you what to do or play mind games."

"I didn't tell you about Jason because I want you to change. I wanted you to understand why I said what I said last night."

"I get it. I have to admit, though, once you said you loved me, well, everything else is a fog."

"I do love you. I love you so much it scares me," Alison whispered her confession.

"Then we'll take it one day at a time." Josh pulled her closer, his head angled, and that kiss, the one she yearned for, poured out of him and became the center of her universe.

Beyond the fence line, dark streams of gold and orange slipped between the trees to end a beautiful day with the promise of an even greater tomorrow.

Epilogue

Six months later ....

Josh and Alison took a ride out on the trail to the spot where the forest widened, and the sunlight slipped through the greens to a fallen tree covering their way.

Josh was the first to dismount and, while holding Destiny's reins, held Gus's bridle for Alison to get down. "Looks like this is the end of the trail."

"It is going to be too heavy to move without going back for tools." Alison looked at the fallen log thoughtfully.

"Later," Josh said, not seeming to worry much about the obstacle Mother Nature left them amid their ride. Alison started to suspect they'd come out here for more than checking the trail.

"We might as well grab the lunch you packed and eat here."

He packed them lunch, and it made her wonder. All summer, she'd been the one to leave the iced tea sun on the porch for them and to ensure Gramps and Josh had a sandwich waiting when they got done working out in the barn and bringing in the hay.

Gramps had offered Josh the permanent position of trail master, and while he healed enough to ride, he seemed content to ride in the back on a sturdy quarter horse he and Josh found a few months back for him to keep company with Maddy and ole Texas.

By the look in Josh's eye, he had more than food on his mind. Alison blushed and walked over to a dry spot under some trees. "It looks dry enough here. Are you sure you want to stop? We'll need to go back and get tools to take care of this before anyone else is stopped by this."

"I'll call Ben. He's got a new chainsaw he's been itching to carve into something. Don't worry. The trail will be clear before Wednesday."

Josh led the horses over and secured them to a thick branch, all the while Alison tried to guess his motive. Josh pulled an extra blanket from the back of his saddle where it had been rolled up and secured to the end.

"What are you up to?"

"This will keep us dry." He rolled it out and placed it in the area she indicated earlier. "I'm told you can't have a picnic without one of these."

Alison giggled. "I thought we came out here to make sure the trail is clean after last night's storm."

"That too."

"Let me guess. Your sister helped you plan this." Alison wasn't at all upset. It delighted her to see he went through so much trouble to spend a little alone time. This was her favorite time of year and, storm or no storm, she was glad they had an excuse to come out on the trail alone.

"Who else?" He gave her his charming smile, the one where his dimple showed, and his eyes twinkled with mischief. It made Alison's stomach flutter.

The summer kept Josh busy with his hauling business, and Alison's brother Scott came to help on the farm. Mom had all but convinced Gramps to go back to Georgia with her, but Scott was the one who decided to transfer his credits and take an internship at the Silver Wind Clinic.

She had a feeling her mother would make more trips back to visit more often, but Alison couldn't deny it made her happy.

Josh reached for the saddlebags. "I can get them."

She couldn't wait to see what kind of surprise Josh had Jenny pack in them. As she pulled out bottles of water and wrapped sandwiches, her smile turned upside down. She laid them out on the blanket and got settled. She had hoped there was more than a meatloaf sandwich inside it.

Trying not to appear too disappointed or anxious, she put her hand in the leather bag one more time.

"Looking for this?"

She glanced over at Josh, and her breath caught in her throat. Bent on one knee, he held out a little blue box, and inside it shimmered a silver banded stone. She couldn't help staring at it, then him, then it again. "Is that what I think it is?"

"It's not the no-bake cookie Jenny stuffed in the other side of the saddlebags for dessert, if that's what you were looking for."

Alison giggled. Those were her favorite, and he remembered those too. She shook her head not sure she could speak.

"Ali, will you take my ring? Will you be my wife?"

Emotions she held for so long clogged her throat and unblocked the wave of joyous tears. She flung herself into Josh's arms, and Josh fell backward. He held onto her as they rolled and Alison laid beneath him. She kissed him hard on the mouth, as if that would be answer enough.

Josh pulled them back up to sitting and took her hand. "Is that a yes? 'Cause I've waited a long time to hear you say it."

"Yes." She laughed and kissed him again.

"What?" he said between kisses.

"I'll be your wife."

Then he grinned because he had to know all along she'd marry him. She watched, her eyes flooding and blurring as she knuckled away the tears, and he slipped the ring on her finger.

"Thank you. Thank you. Thank you!" Josh tucked her close to him.

"You were afraid I'd say no?" She hadn't known for sure until a few weeks ago. Watching Jenny and Cade with their new son as a family had once more made her dream of what it'd be like for her and Josh to have a family of their own and had pushed her heart in the right direction. Or maybe it was the lack of little girls, with all those boys who would be running around Silver Wind. Either way, God had timed it all perfectly.

A Special Thanks

Thank you for reading along with Sarah, Jenny, and Josh at the Silver Wind Equine Rescue Ranch.

If you would please take a moment and review this book, I and other readers would greatly appreciate it

Want more books in this series? I'd love to hear your thoughts. Be sure to drop me a line at my website: susanlower.com

Sign up for my newsletter at susalower.com and never miss a new release. I've even got a free book for you and I randomly have giveaways.

Susan Lower

Other Books By Susan

Silver Wind Equine Rescue Romances
Forgotten Reins
Unbridled
Silver Stirrups

The Brides of Annie Creek Novella Series
The Fruitcake Bride
The Thimble Bride
The Postage Stamp Bride

Hearts of Hidden Hills
Residence of Her Heart
Salvaged Hearts

Planet Mitch Series for Kids ages 7 – 12
The Lost Star — Book One
Blast Off — Book Two
The Black Eyed Galaxy — Book Three

Made in the USA
Coppell, TX
30 May 2020